Love

SEAGULL
BOOKS
•
CELEBRATING
40 YEARS

TOMAS ESPEDAL

Love

TRANSLATED BY
JAMES ANDERSON

LONDON NEW YORK CALCUTTA

Seagull Books, 2022

First published in Norwegian as *Elsken* by Tomas Espedal
© Gyldendal Norsk Forlag, 2018

First published in English translation by Seagull Books, 2022
English translation © James Anderson, 2022

This translation has been published with
the financial support of NORLA

ISBN   978 1 8030 9 080 1

British Library Cataloguing-in-Publication Data
A catalogue record for this book is available from the British Library.

Typeset by Seagull Books, Calcutta, India
Printed and bound in USA by Integrated Books International

Death is good when it comes like a lover.

Pierre Jean Jouve

I is searching for a place to die. He falls, gets to his feet, brushes the earth from his clothes, looks up at the trees: green leaves and needles, pine and spruce interspersed with birch and ash, and occasionally aspen; heart-shaped, wing-shaped leaves, as if the trees, these hard, upright, lonely tree trunks were seeking out shapes in nature which they could imitate and occasionally embrace, as when a squirrel leaps from branch to branch, or a bird settles in the crown of a tree and sings out lustily: morning's here!

Each and every leaf is unique. And yet not, the leaves grow together and clothe the tree like a unifying thought: we are the tree. The tree is us. We are spring, summer and autumn. In the winter we're gone, laid beneath the soil. Dead and overgrown. In the winter we dissolve. The winter is when we die. I curses. He's damp with earth and mud. Only seen by birds and passed on by them like gossip, from bough to bough and then on wings and so-called song to distant places. Distant places aren't always far enough away. But she can't understand the tell-tale song of the birds. Or can she? Will she hear about his fall? I sings. He's merry at the thought of his impending death. But where to die? In the forest or by the sea? In the mountains? Or in the suburbs on the way to the city? In a car park? It's important to find the right place. A forest clearing with a river running through it. No. This isn't the right place. Perhaps a garden. Apple trees and raspberry bushes. Roses. Jasmine and hawthorn hedges, a brook and a slope, waterfalls and birds again, always birds, always restlessness. Always gossip and rumour. Hardly ever silence. I is searching for silence. A quiet place. Home? A bed. In bed with sleeping tablets. It'll be a long sleep. A good sleep. Are you asleep? No. I'm not asleep. He's awake and dreaming. Just to lie on your back, on pine needles or in bed, and dream! To live, to dream, it's the same thing. He's spent his life dreaming. Even standing up. Even walking. And there, in the midst of the dream, like a fly in a spider's web, was life. Shiny, soft, sparkling life. Hard life, transparent, like a fly's wing, struggling, attached to the pulsating body of a fly that's soon devoured by a small, black creature. Death. It can be so beautiful. Life, too, can be beautiful. When, of necessity, life and death come together, there's a moment of natural beauty. One must create this beauty for oneself. One must submit to this naturalness, one must choose it, like pulling the duvet over oneself in bed or jumping off a bridge. One falls asleep, or sinks, that's natural. These are I's thoughts as he walks down to the sea, the cove close to where he lives; down through what they call

5

LOVE

Utnehagen to where the scrub and brush give way to a smoother, harder place in which the grass yields to flat rocks and boulders at the edge of the water, blue.

I walks to the sea. He undresses, folds his clothes painstakingly into a pile. These clothes, how beautiful they are. The shirt, the trousers, the boots. Dirty. These clothes, so full of life. There they lie by the water's edge breathing. I swims. He stretches out his arms and legs, pulls his arms and legs in, back, gathering his body. Floats. Increases speed. Out with his arms and legs. Breathe in and out. Swallow water. Sink here? I sinks. He swims under water. Black. No. Not here. Not dirty or clean enough. Not blue enough. Do you remember? I remembers. He remembers the blue of the sea at Kas. The tip of Turkey. Her and him on holiday. There. On the beach. In the sun. The heat. Beads of perspiration beneath her eyes. Now she's eating an apricot. Later, in the evening, in the light from the paper lanterns; an orange. One incision with her fruit knife and she removed the orange rind in one long peel. Almost like violence. How did you do that, manage that? It's no big deal, I'm eating fruit, it's natural. She was natural. Where did she get it from? Didn't she have parents? Had she sprung out of someone's head, fully dressed? All these clothes. He put them on and took them off. The smell of dressing. The smell of undressing. The smell of her. One can fall in love with a smell. One can become dependent on a smell. It clings to her clothes and then gradually to objects, to furniture, to curtains and carpets, the smell wafts out into the rooms, and soon she fills the entire house. The house smells good. It smells of love. It doesn't take long for the smell to permeate you as well. It has become your own. You smell of her. Your smell is a mixture of you and her, and that's the smell of love. Her armpits, your sex, your sweat, her blood, it all mixes. Your life and hers. In a common smell. How can you live without her? How can you live? How can you live without love? I thinks this as he swims in the cold sea. Pushing water aside and remembering. Sink, rise, swallow water. The taste of salt. The taste of death. No. It's the taste of life. I swims to the shore. He crawls out of the water on all fours and feels the warmth of the sea rocks and the warmth of the sun. I lies on his stomach on the round rock and feels the warmth, lays his cold palms on the hard stone, feels how he's being heated through and gets a powerful erection.

I has tried to live alone. He's travelled, he's visited countries and cities. He's eaten at restaurants and drunk in bars. He's known boredom. He's sought friendship. He's had girlfriends. What Susa called little love affairs. If we're lucky we have one big love affair, and some little love affairs, Susa said, sitting on a high bar stool. Stiletto heels, long stockings, a full-length coat, everything about her was attenuated, and to add to this stature she was wearing a hat. Susa had been with 63 men. She'd made a list of their names. After each name she'd put a colon, and then noted the approximate length of the owner's erect penis. Together with certain characteristics, like: Kind. Gullible. Unintelligent. Spiteful. Jealous. Amusing. Talkative. Things like that. Susa had written books. She was a wise man, or more properly a wise woman, but women are stupid, Susa said, it's our job to take care of stupidity. I no longer concern myself with sex and age, she said, they're artificial concepts, sometimes I'm a boy of 19, but just now I'm a woman of 73. You shouldn't deny yourself the little love affairs, she said. I've been celibate. They were the best years. Without men. Without women. Without sexual relations, it makes sexuality broader, loftier, one comes to love trees and birds, clouds and flowers, children and old people, one comes to love life. And the most important thing I discovered is that when one loves many people, when desire is no longer fixed on one particular individual whom one must own or be owned by, whom one must possess or be possessed by, one sits amongst friends or strangers and thinks I love them all. I love the community. I love people. For good or ill. I once knew a cannibal. He ate the one he loved. That was in Paris. Montaigne thought cannibals were civilized. They only kill what they can eat. In our so-called civilization we take life by the hundred thousand. People and animals. I met Borges.

I wanted to look nice for him. One of my women friends, this was in Buenos Aires, said: Why are you getting tarted up? Borges is blind. I put on my best clothes. Earrings and hat. Makeup. A silk scarf. A dab of perfume. A special item of jewellery. When I was shown into his work room, by his mother, Borges was sitting behind his desk in semi-darkness, he said: What lovely clothes you're wearing.

I has dressed up too. He doesn't want to die looking scruffy. He got up early, showered, shaved and got out his best suit; dark jacket and trousers, a white shirt, dark tie, he dressed as one might dress for a funeral, his own funeral, the way it would have been in his imagination, in a chapel, filled with people. He was at a funeral only a fortnight ago; it was pretty much the kind he'd have liked himself: family and friends, a whole lot of acquaintances and some visitors. He'd arrived with Aka, they were late, they'd been drinking and making love the night before and overslept, phoned for a taxi, got dressed at top speed and were driven to the chapel which was already full, they had to walk up the aisle in full view, like a black-clad, ill-kempt bridal pair, all the way up to the second pew, where there were spare seats behind the grieving family.

There were two good eulogies, loud weeping, Aka wept too even though she hadn't known the deceased. The piano was played, some Grieg, some Bach; it put I in mind of a line from one of the cantatas: *Ich freue mich auf meinen Tod*. I took Aka's hand, they sat in the chapel holding hands, was this a beginning or an end? Why aren't you crying? Aka whispered. I didn't cry at funerals, he didn't know why, perhaps his relationship with death was too intimate, he didn't necessarily think it was sad when someone died. At least not if the deceased had really lived. Karel had been a year younger than himself, and he'd lived an intense life, a rich life, as one of Karel's friends I knew this. And death might be a good thing, it was conceivable and perfectly possible. It was a Christian funeral, and in the Christian faith death is better than life. It was precisely this that the priest emphasized: that the deceased had now come home. Karel who for most of his life had been moving about or travelling, who in many ways had made himself constructively homeless, had now come home. To a good place. A permanent place. He had, it was to be hoped, settled down.

They bore Karel out of the chapel in a white coffin. The coffin was heavy. Karel was tall and would certainly have tipped the scales at 14 stone. A couple of the pallbearers were already flagging on the first slope leading to his appointed resting place. The bearers had problems carrying the coffin and, as they turned a corner and headed for the second slope, they dropped it; it struck the asphalt and over-turned, the coffin lid flew off and out rolled Karel, he practically flung himself out of his coffin. He rolled over twice before coming to rest on his back, quite alive, so it seemed, or sleeping, just like himself, just as people remembered seeing him so many times asleep on a sofa. A cry rose from the long cortège which stood as if paralysed, horrified at how lifelike the corpse looked. He was himself, just paler, a bit thinner, and dressed in the clothes he liked to go about in. It was easy to imagine him sitting up and brushing the dirt from his clothes, as he'd done once when he'd been on the ground after a fight, and then rolling over and getting to his feet to cadge a cigarette. But now everyone could see that Karel was dead. They saw death. They understood what death was, it was brutal, it was a total absence of life. They realized that Karel would never get up again, not even in an afterlife. Karel's brothers and nephews rushed up and managed to get the corpse back into the coffin. It was raised by a new, stronger set of bearers and laid across the rectangular hole in the ground, and the wreaths were laid along the edge of the grave. Then the coffin was lowered with cords into the ground.

The sun was shining the day I left home, it was a lovely day. I had a good breakfast, toast and eggs. A cup of coffee. Then he put on a coat, laced up his black walking boots, laced them up tightly and left, he had no plans to return.

How odd it felt shutting your own door for the last time. Closing the door. Should you lock it, no, you'll leave the door open. As always. As never again. All your things are here in the house, the chairs you love so much, the lamps, the bookcases, the books. All these books that live inside you. All those words and sentences, names and places that live inside you. Even the furniture and the knickknacks live inside you; some of the furniture was handed down by your parents and grandparents, some of the objects were presents from friends and girlfriends, and you want to take them with you to where you're going. The objects will be discarded or sold, the furniture cleared away and the house will stand empty. An empty house. Until it's filled up once more. Your home will be destroyed. In the same way that you'll be destroyed. You'll have gone just like the furniture and the bits and pieces and the home. It's natural. You'll have gone just like everything you loved, like all the people you loved, will be gone. All your life, ever since you were a child, you've relished the idea of being able to vanish. It's been your freedom, your secret, your trait: that vanishing thing. You could disappear in front of your parents' eyes and at a children's party and in a classroom and there right beside your girlfriend, she was holding your hand, but you weren't there. So where were you? You were absent. So where were you? You were absent somewhere that only exists as a non-existence, an away place, you were with death. Early in life you were with death. It was a good place. It was where you came from and where you were going, and it was the place that followed you all your life, and in which you could seek sanctuary, at any time. It was your place. This unknown. This other place.

This was where I was going now, today.

Just as I was closing the door, he heard a voice, it was his neighbour. I lived in a terrace of four small houses and he had good neighbours, and now, as so often before, he heard his next-door neighbour's voice, he generally heard this voice muffled by walls, he found it soothing to be sur-rounded by voices, by noises, from his neighbours' lives, but occasionally these voices detached themselves from their hidden and confined existences and came straight at him, outside the house, and that made him anxious, as if he were guilty of something, he was unprotected and defenceless; had he been ambushed, no, he hadn't, but even so he shut his ears as if invisibly recreating the walls that divided him from his neighbours; he always took what was inside the house with him whenever he went out. It was Rank's voice. It cut through the air, the fresh morning air: Are you off to a funeral? I stood for a moment unsure of what to say. He was in his best clothes. It was only eight or nine o'clock: No, he said at last, I'm going to a party. One of your morn-ing parties, Rank said. They laughed. I led an irregular life, everyone knew that. By the way, it's your turn to mow the grass, Rank said, it's Saturday tomorrow, maybe you could cut the grass then, if you survive your party, before Sunday arrives, the day of rest.

I's conscience was pricked. He couldn't very well depart without cutting the grass, without fulfilling his obligations. On the other hand, if he were to fulfil all his obligations, there would never be time to die. Was he to be delayed, perhaps even prevented, by trifles? Wasn't this monthly grass cutting just a trifle, a middle-class fad, a decorative duty; it irritated him; he'd have let the grass grow wild, left the crocuses and dandelions in peace, let the weeds and wild flowers stand unmolested, but it wasn't his grass, not his lawn, it belonged to the Residents' Association.

I peeled off his coat, went to the tool shed and got out the lawnmower. Walk up and down in straight lines, decapitate flowers, cut grass that's already short, walk up and down, sweat—he liked this walking to and fro on the lawn, but he didn't like the thought of cutting the grass, slicing off the yellow dandelion heads, or the orchid-like cress (which his mother loved so much) and especially the clover flowers which were so vital for the bees (but who thought of the bees in this Residents' Association which was so fixated on superficialities, on facades, on everything that was contrary to nature; in concert they tried to eradicate slugs, poison was put out for rats, cats were chased away and spiders' webs removed, they smoked out wasps' nests, gassed ants and insects, all these small creatures that we basically depend on), and I liked bees, he was fond of wasps and spiders, ants and earthworms, everything that lived in the earth and grew up out of it, an unending cycle of growth and life which was disrupted by this mowing, just as we disrupt nature in almost everything we do, I thought. In almost everything he did now, and in everything he wasn't going to do from now on, I attempted to justify his own death. I ought to say that I don't agree with this cruel grass cutting, I thought, and do it today, the last day, I thought as he went on mowing the grass. I ought to leave the grass uncut, but I'm taking my turn at tidying up, for the last time. Perhaps I ought to leave half the lawn untouched, to make my point, my protest; people will see what I thought about all this mowing, I thought.

Ever since I had lived next door to Rank, Rank had been a good neighbour, a normal neighbour you might say; when I had moved into the terrace, Rank had been in love, she'd moved in with him, they'd had a daughter, and when this daughter turned 14, Rank and Arie got divorced, she moved out, that was normal. Most of the things about the neighbourhood and the Residents' Association were normal; the lights were turned on and off at the correct times.

People married and got divorced when necessary. But after Rank was left on his own, he developed the habit of renovating his house, room by room, three storeys, cellar and lounge, kitchen and bathroom, the bedrooms on the top floor, wall after wall, door after door, and the stairs between the floors, it seemed as if it were some everlasting project with its stripping and banging, drilling and din. Rank was a quiet and even-tempered man, but the divorce and his new solitary life didn't seem to have done him any good; the thumping and boring went on in the evenings, after work, and often on Saturdays and Sundays, it was as if there were no rest days any more, there on the other side of the wall, and that Rank, behind the thin partition that separated him and I, had turned into an inconsiderate and raucous ogre, noisy at all hours of the day, the good neighbour was becoming, without knowing it, because I never complained, he hated confrontation and wouldn't for all the world be on bad terms with Rank, with his neighbour, Rank was becoming a foe, almost an enemy. Rank had undergone a metamorphosis, there, right behind the wall; I was very disturbed by this new Rank, by the banging and especially the drilling which transplanted itself from the brick walls and into I's head.

It was as if Rank had moved into I's life. I felt forced to think about Rank, who was Rank? I didn't want to know, but had no choice but to think about Rank anyway, had to consider that Rank, despite all his affability and veneer of good neighbourliness wasn't, perhaps, a good person. Why didn't Rank show any consideration for I, to the consideration that I showed Rank, to I's lack of noise, his quietness and near silence compared to Rank? I wanted to be on good terms with his neighbours. I wanted a detached relationship with his neighbours. Might Rank's inconsiderate behaviour be a result of this, revenge perhaps, might Rank's commotion be revenge for I's silence? This thought disturbed I's private life, threatened it; and I had, for the first time since he'd come to the terrace, thought about moving; but where could he move to?

I lived in his childhood home. He loved living in the house where nothing had changed since he was a child growing up there. I had altered nothing; the wallpaper and carpets were the same, the furniture; he'd moved a few tables and chairs, and that was all.

I had lived in other places, for some years abroad, for some years in his home town, in various flats, but when his parents died, in quick succession, they'd lived almost all their lives together and they died together, which seemed natural, and it was just as natural for I to move into the dead couple's house, into his childhood home. He'd found his place. The place where he belonged. The place where he felt happy.

You move and search, you travel and stay, without finding the place where you want to settle. And if you ultimately find the place, your place, the place where you want to be, where everything comes together and where you're content; *the* place; a place where you settle down and can fulfil your potential, well, that's a gift; here you can do what you were meant to do, and in I's case that was writing, he'd written and published several books and for much of his writing career he'd been searching for a place that could unlock the best in him, the most important work, the place where he could concentrate sufficiently to write better than he'd done up till then, a major work, if you like. And he'd found that place; it was rather like coming full circle; what you'd thought of as far off, in a different place, the perfect place, was quite close at hand, almost at the beginning, where you'd begun your search, and for I that meant where he'd begun to write; he now wrote in the room where he'd started writing when he was 16.

I mowed half the lawn with the petrol mower, cut the engine and pushed the machine back to the tool shed. For a moment he considered getting into his car, in the garage, starting the engine and sitting there, in the dark, in the car, with the windows down, listening to music on the radio; until everything went silent at last.

But no, it was too early, too soon, he still had the whole day in front of him, and it really was a lovely day, the sun shone, the sky was lofty and the light so blue amongst all the greenery that sprang from the earth or the trees. I wanted to go for a walk, he wanted to inhale the day in all its mass and beauty. There are two sweet extremities in all experience, and they are 'for the first and the last time': the first time you see a tree, the first time you kiss, the first time you make love and the last time you make love, the last time you drink a cup of coffee, the last time you see a tree: See the tree! Now taste the coffee! Hey, you're making love! Whereas most of the times in between have become habitual and you don't see what you're looking at, your woman, your coffee cup, the front door, the gravel path, the garden gate; you walk past the playschool without even noticing it, you don't even see the rhododendron bushes around the car park, or the people getting in and out of their cars, you don't see the houses or the windows you pass, all that's become commonplace for you, and maybe you're tired of everyday things, you're not interested in them, or they irritate you, you're irritated by the cars and the traffic and all the noise and stupidity that goes on during the course of a day. The day has slipped away from you. You've lost your faith in the day, in the first and the last, in the newness that's to be found in every day, that's to be found in every beginning and ending. A new day. It does exist, but you don't see it, your day is like other days, this is because you're already dead. Something inside you is dead. When did it die, when did you die, was it when love ended? One cannot live without love. And yet you live, a half life, an almost life, a dead life is what you're living. Such thoughts left I feeling high-flown and excited, they confirmed that the decision he'd taken was right: that exquisite decision to die.

I wanted to die the good death. Not the sort that arrives without warning or by accident, or as an illness, not the death you push away and deny, but the death you choose and go out to meet. I wanted to die while he was still full of vitality and of sound mind, he wanted to die on a day when he was feeling satisfied and at ease. It was a year since I had made his big decision, and he'd known that this final year would be like no other. He'd made no plans and would take the year as it came, as a gift. He'd known nothing about the year ahead, except that it would be the last. The last July, the last August and autumn, winter and spring, the last week, and the last days, like a countdown to, and intensification of, the day that was today.

I had come to his decision in the spring, on a warm spring day in May; he was lying on the patio reading in the sun. The decision had lain there inside him ever since Vali left, that was almost six years ago; and he'd lived alone during those years. He liked living alone. It was a novelty for him to live alone, but even that had become a habit now and he had no desire for anything new; a new relationship, a new journey, new projects, all this was dead to him, and the decision to end it all had grown and matured within him until it finally blossomed like some interior bloom, black and beautiful, in May, one warm day on the patio.

Only a few days after he took his decision, I was invited to France. Some friends had rented a gîte in the Loire, in the little village of Candé-sur-Beuvron. Seven friends in a large house in France; he made up his mind to go, bought a plane ticket, one way, packed his rucksack and dug out his old walking boots, put on his black wool suit, a white shirt, and flew to Paris. He took a train from Paris to Orleans and then to Blois, where Dreas picked him up in a hire car. They drove by the side of the river. Dreas was happy, played French music on the car radio, drove fast, sang and smoked: Dreas with his short, red hair, sunglasses, pale blue shirt, white trousers, he said, 'Everyone's arrived, you're the last.' Dreas said, 'Rie, Nille, Aka, Dun, Enning, they're all waiting for us in the garden, we've laid a big table, we'll eat and drink and enjoy the good life.'

The house had formerly been a hostel, two storeys high, two large living rooms and a kitchen on the ground floor, the bedrooms up above. I was given a dark red room with

a bed and a writing table. Mirror and wash basin. Bedside
table. Lamp. A glass door lead to a small patio overgrown
with hawthorn and wild raspberries. The friends were sitting at a long table in the garden at the back of the house.
I knew them all, apart from Rie and Aka. He kept aloof
from the two women, just as he kept his distance from all
his friends. I was not a devotee of friendship. He liked being
with this group of friends and enjoyed observing them from
the patio, or from his corner of the table, and when they
took their daily stroll along the river, he walked a couple of
paces behind the others, it was only in the evenings, when
they'd eaten and drunk, when they were mellow, that he
lost his reserve and got drawn into the warm, soft companionship of voices and movements; at night they danced,
beneath the strings of lights that had been hung up between
the fruit trees in the garden.

I had never enjoyed such a lovely week as this week
with friends. Now it was over. They were going home. I had
no return ticket. He decided to walk from Blois to Paris, it
was roughly a week's hike, he wanted to walk along the river
and through the forests towards Versailles and Paris. On the
final evening, while they were having dinner round the big
table in the garden, he asked, almost as a joke, if anyone
wanted to come along, if anyone wanted to walk to Paris
with him. And to his great surprise Aka said yes, she'd

accompany him to Paris. I instantly regretted his lack of restraint, his sentimentality. Wouldn't it be better for him to go alone? He was in love. In love from afar. He wanted to maintain that distance. He wanted to choke off the feeling of love; it would subside anyway once they left the house, once they returned to their own homes; but now they'd be walking to Paris together. Did Aka know what she was letting herself in for? They'd be spending a week together, walking along country roads, perhaps sleeping in the open, they'd be thrown into close proximity.

In the morning Dreas drove them to the railway station at Blois, and there they found themselves, suddenly, standing side by side their packs on their backs. Aka with her wild black hair, her unpainted face, her beautiful eyes; was there fear in those eyes? Just for an instant, during an exchanged glance, I thought let's forget this terrible walking trip; take the train, get the whole thing over, say goodbye to each other in Paris and go our separate ways. Then they began to walk. Towards Mer, the nearest village, 14 miles away. They walked by the river. The sun was shining. It was hot. They peeled off their clothes, walked in T-shirts and shorts. They didn't talk, walked in silence along the track that accompanied the river as it snaked its way shiny and cool through the flat landscape of cornfields and meadows, interrupted only by farmsteads and livestock; occasionally birds, they flew up, black, like in a painting by van Gogh. Aka was an actor, she'd studied philosophy, she seldom spoke about herself. There was a stillness about her. Now she retreated into this stillness; she almost vanished into it, right there next to him, he really liked it: the way she almost walked by herself, alone, she walked so beautifully, he thought. They passed a farm, a garden with fruit trees: I picked two apples, some plums, they sat in the shade under a lime tree and ate, drank water. They lay side by side in the grass, resting. Talked a bit about the need for bees, the colours of butterflies, the beauty of wild flowers, about the sound of grasshoppers. They reached Mer in the evening. Found a hotel called Felicidad where there was just one vacant room, a small room with a double bed. They slept next to each other in the darkness. In the morning they had breakfast at the hotel before carrying on towards Beaugency. A new day walking by the River Loire. Another night in a hotel room. I lay awake for a long time wondering how many nights he'd manage to lie next to her like this, without touching her. She slept with her back towards him. He'd seen her naked now; she was so lovely that it was painful to lie behind her, sleepless, hot. In the morning they decided to take the bus to Chartres, they wanted to see the cathedral. Their aching and blistered feet needed to recuperate. They rested at Chartres, at the Hôtel de Poèmes, in a little, blue room with yellow curtains. In the evening they went out to see the

cathedral, it was lit up by a play of lights that projected char-
acters and colours on to its facade; and for the first time
they cried together, they stood in front of the cathedral and
cried. They were together without being together. They
were together without making love, that was how it was.
They slept and walked together, they ate and drank together,
they talked and laughed together, but they didn't touch one
another, and it was lovely, it was hard.

Over the next three days they walked the route to
Versailles. They followed the river before striking off north-
wards, walking through forests and areas of open farmland,
past villages and hamlets, towards the city, the capital, Paris.
At Versailles they spent two nights at the Hôtel d'Angleterre,
not far from the palace which they visited on Saturday: in
the palace halls I spent the whole time watching Aka who
was looking at paintings and wall hangings, carpets and fabrics, furniture and beds, lamps and mirrors; he studied her
almost as one studies a work of art, something you can never
own. Something you covet, but can never have. Something
you love but can never possess; it was as if Aka was transformed by the rooms she passed through, by the things she
looked at; she didn't belong to him, but to these gilded mirrors, these colourful fabrics, these expensive beds; all this
lent her a peculiar beauty, it was as if now, in these Versailles
halls, he'd fallen in love with something unattainable. He

lost her, she became invisible to him, there at Versailles; and yet he got more and more fond of her, yes, he loved her now; he was on his way to being unhappy.

On Saturday they were to do the last stage, from Versailles to Paris. It was also the loveliest leg: the city lay there like a slumbering animal, you couldn't see it, but you sensed its closeness: a special luminosity in the sky, a distant hum, and suddenly, at the top of a rise, there, behind the forest and all the scenery that's saturated your vision during a week of walking: you see the city. You see the city as something unsettling and beautiful in the distance. You see the city as something dangerous and savage, as a different kind of nature; brutal. It was as if they hung back from going down the other side of the hill, down towards the city, while at the same time they felt the city's attraction; it lay over there and waited for them.

They crossed the Seine at Severe, walked to the nearest metro station and took the tube to Bastille and the Hôtel Baudin where I had put up on several occasions; he'd written parts of a novel at the window of the small hotel room, that had been 11 years ago, and he hadn't been here since then; that was in a different life.

You die several times in the course of a lifetime. I couldn't even recall who he'd been the first time he came to Paris. There were several cities called Paris inside him;

now the city was new as he walked by Aka's side and viewed its streets as an extension of her, it was as if the city lay in the shadow of her back and hair.

That evening they ate at Chez Paul, close to the hotel. They sat at a small table outside the restaurant, on the pavement, boxed in by other tables, between Parisians who were eating and drinking; Aka in her black jacket, loose black trousers, her long dark hair gathered in a ponytail. They each had a juicy steak and they drank two bottles of wine. In bed that night, Aka stretched out her hand towards him, scarcely touching him, it was the first time.

On Sunday they went to an exhibition at the Jeu de Paume: 'La vie folle', a collection of photographs by Ed van der Elsken. They took the metro to Place de la Concorde, queued for tickets to an exhibition neither of them was prepared for; they didn't know van der Elsken's work. The photographs were mainly studies in black and white, exhibited in bright rooms. They went round separately: I didn't want to blend his emotions with Aka's, didn't want to share his loneliness with hers but gradually, as he looked at the pictures, the photos of couples making love, of vulnerable lovers in the nocturnal life of Amsterdam and Paris; rough sleepers, prostitutes, artists and vagabonds; men kissing women, women clasping men, men and women who danced, who made love, who lived and drank in the night;

the more pictures he saw, the greater his yearning grew for
Aka who was moving amongst the photographs; he couldn't
distinguish her from the people he saw in the pictures, the
lovers, and all he wanted was to live like them, with Aka;
weren't she and he already like the subjects in the photographs, hadn't they the same faces, and weren't they already
a couple, a van der Elsken couple? There was a moment
when he went across and kissed Aka's neck. Could she see
what he saw? She turned and kissed him on the mouth.
They kissed. They stood amongst the pictures of the lovers
and kissed. It was the photographs which unleashed the kiss,
which turned them into lovers, they became lovers in front
of the pictures of lovers; it was as if a world opened up in
the rooms of photographs, a world of possibility, everything
was possible, even love, always, everywhere.

I had lost faith in a new love, nor did he want one; but here
in the gallery, amongst the van der Elsken photographs,
standing behind Aka, who suddenly turned and kissed him,
he was struck by something unexpected, like a bolt of lightning, or a shaft of light, as if the light from the photographs
flashed into his eyes and exposed an inner picture, a picture
of Aka and himself as lovers, as a couple; he was filled with
a yearning for love. The beggars and poor people captured
on film, people without anything, had love.

Aka and I left the exhibition, walked the streets of Paris, traipsed aimlessly round the city as if they were vagrants, homeless, poor, as if they were lovers now. They walked along the bank of the Seine, under the bridges, found a river boat where they ate and drank wine. The sun went down behind Notre-Dame. They felt cold and took a taxi to the hotel. Sat side by side in the back seat and watched the street lights coming on. In the hotel room, with the curtains open, they made love in the faint glow from the city.

In the morning I accompanied Aka to the railway station, she was going to the airport and flying home. When she disappeared down the escalator, it felt as if she'd gone for ever: I couldn't rid himself of the thought that perhaps he'd never see her again. He was in love. He was in love with Aka. That was the truth. He walked all the way from the Gare d'Austerlitz to Bastille, to the Hôtel Baudin where he went to bed for two days. He was sick. Lovesick. It was a good sickness, it gave him the desire to live. Perhaps this was the right moment to die, just as he was at his happiest, just as he had the greatest will to live? Should he end it all here, in his hotel room in Paris? It would be a romantic death, perfect in its beauty. A brief letter on the writing table. The letter to Aka. A love letter. Lying on the bed in his suit and boots. Dressed for a final journey. As always, I had his bottle of sleeping tablets close at hand, with his washing things; he went out to the bathroom. Looked at himself in the mirror. He seemed younger. His face was a healthy colour from the sun and the trek from the Loire. He swallowed a sleeping pill, almost as a foretaste, and drank a glass of water. Then he got into bed. After a few terrible hours of torment and doubt, he finally fell asleep with his arms around Aka's duvet.

On Wednesday I took the plane from Paris to Berlin where he spent the night near the railway station before taking the train onward to Hamburg and Copenhagen. He liked sitting on a train, making notes in a notebook, reading a newspaper, drinking bottles of wine and eating, sleeping by the window which moved so pleasantly past featureless landscape; what had he dreamt about? At Hamburg the carriage suddenly filled with people, women and men, wailing children. They piled into the carriage and completely packed it; everyone squeezed up. One heard the word refugees. A stream of refugees. I sat hemmed in by a family and all its possessions, packs and bags, holdalls and suitcases which filled the coach with a smell of desperation and flight: in the course of just a few minutes the peaceful carriage had been transformed into a scene of battle; one sat amongst people who'd witnessed war. Who'd seen their homes being levelled. Who'd seen their loved ones die. I sat pressed up against people who'd fled from death. They were travelling away from death. He was travelling towards it. I sat pressed up against people who wanted to live, who'd sacrificed everything for that one thing: to live. These migrants had nothing, apart from life. Precious life. I sat amongst the refugees and travelled in the opposite direction: he travelled towards death, the death he'd chosen. Wasn't he ashamed of himself? He who had everything, a home, a girlfriend, work. No, he wasn't ashamed. For a few hours, in the railway carriage between Hamburg and Copenhagen, squashed in amongst the refugees, he felt a strong desire to live. These travellers had left death behind them, he had death before him, and it was this closeness to death that kindled in him the desire to live, that allowed him to see and feel: he saw people around him, he felt their misery and desperation sponta- neously; he wanted so much to help them, and during the journey he turned over the thought that he ought to offer his home to the family seated around him. Should he do it? A father and a mother, two small girls, they needed what he wanted to leave, a home. I put the words together, rehearsed the sentences, let them fly around in his thoughts; he was close to exhaustion by the time the train approached Copenhagen, but he couldn't manage to say: 'You are wel- come to my home.' He wanted to say it. He couldn't get the words out, something inside him kept the words back, as if they were shut in, by fear? What did he fear? I looked at the two girls. They were his girls too, his responsibility, they were sitting right in front of him, they needed help. I could help them. But he didn't do it. He sat there silent. He needed a home to die in. Was his death more important than their life? The family's life, the girls' future? No. But there was a fear within him, he discovered it now on the train to Copenhagen: he wasn't frightened of death, he was frightened of life.

In Copenhagen I looked up his friend Karel. Karel had moved out of Bergen and rented a flat in Viktoriagade. A corner flat on the top floor of the block with a view of the old meat market at Vesterbro: a flat Karel had filled with books and lamps. He was a reader. And a writer. Karel had dedicated his life to reading and writing. He lived alone. The flat bore witness to isolation and the life of the cloister; a small monk's cell in the heart of the city; Karel was celibate. He considered that celibacy afforded him a special concentration and calm; he spent his time and energy working; he was writing a book about Francis of Assisi. All those years alone had given Karel a spiritual radiance, he'd become pale and almost transparent, as if his white skin was a thin membrane constantly penetrated by the dead and the living, he lived like a ghost amongst ghosts; he didn't seem to have attained any specific age. His long, fair hair was curly, he was a beautiful man, he looked like a woman.

Karel's manuscripts were in longhand. He wrote in pencil, a thin, almost illegible handwriting; tiny letters squeezed together in sentences that resembled waves in a kind of aquatic script: One should read and forget, Karel said. He spoke softly, like a singer who over many years has perfected his voice to emphasize only the essence of a song line: you heard fragments of what he said, certain words that stood out like deep growls in muttering; he didn't talk, he sang. Karel sang. I had to concentrate to stop himself nodding off. He'd be woken by foreign words, German ones or French ones, occasionally Spanish and Dutch: Karel was on a journey and now the two friends were in a dream about Amsterdam: the canals . . . the light . . . the muddy puddles . . . the clouds . . . the pigeons . . . the grey colour . . . good boots . . . drowning . . . doors . . . hearing . . . another place . . . quiet . . . greyer . . . the footsteps . . . birds and children . . . hiding places . . . stairs . . . the voices . . . the trees . . . the shadows . . . sunlight . . . the face . . . snowfalls . . . weddings . . . all time . . . under water.

I woke up and wanted to tell Karel about his resolution, but Karel got in first and said that he was ill. Karel wouldn't put a name to the disease, he had no faith in names, he said; they

reinforce more than they define, we go by so many names;
I'm called happy and sad, one day I'm called that lucky man,
another day Karel and another day my name has gone.

And the illness will vanish too, he said.

I could call the illness life.

I could call the illness love.

I could call the illness Karel.

It's the names that kill us, Karel told I.

The two friends breakfasted together before Karel accompanied I to the door: I'd rather not go out, he said. I make my journeys within the flat. I get my food delivered by courier. I've got a good bed. I remember and forget with equal curiosity. Sleep is a huge territory. My illness has taught me to love life. The simple, quiet life. I used to be tired, and now I'm alert. I have no greater wish than to live, said Karel and kissed I on the mouth.

I took the suburban line from Central Station to Nordhavnen and then walked the mile to the Oslo ferry dock. He was allotted a cabin in the bowels of the boat. He sat on deck watching their departure from Copenhagen. He had a gin and tonic. He had a cigarette. He read a novel for a while. He ate in the Italian restaurant. He was disturbed

by a man who talked to him as if they were old acquaintances. He hadn't the faintest idea who the man was. Alfdan,
the man prompted, but it didn't help, the name meant
nothing. He went out on to the side deck, by the lifeboats
for a cigarette. But he had to stub it out and go straight back
in: as he stood at the rail he felt a sudden draw from the sea,
a powerful impulse to throw himself into the cold, dark
water. Simply vanish into the foaming waves. He had to put
out his cigarette and practically jump back, away from the
rail and its lure, and return to the restaurant where he had
a glass of grappa and paid his bill. He walked to the stern of
the boat, to the bar and dance floor. He ordered a whisky,
sat down at a table with a view of the band and the dancers.
He liked to watch the people dancing. He enjoyed the raucous dance music. There was music by Abba. By Smokie.
By Dr Hook. He liked such music. He sat watching the
band, three men and two women. He studied the dancers'
shoes and feet, the dancers' footwork, the quick movement
of their feet across the floor, to the rhythm of the bass and
drums. I had once been a boxer. In another life. How many
lives do we live? I'm not the same person I was then, there
are at least three or four people between us, I thought. He
ordered another drink from the waiter who was moving
between the tables. I was happy on board the Oslo ferry.
He looked forward to sleeping deep inside the boat, in the
cabin without windows; hearing the sound of the engine

thumping like a heart, in the darkness; the gentle rocking as
he lay curled up in the foetal position.

I wanted to visit Vali in Oslo. He wanted to see her one last
time. Would she see him? He sent a text from his phone:
I'm in Oslo. Would like to meet. Ok by you? I had breakfast
on the boat. He sat at the window in the dining room and
watched them dock in Oslo. From Oslo he'd take the night
train to Bergen. He had a whole day and evening in the
city: this'll be the last time in Oslo, the last time with Vali,
he thought. But then she sent him a text saying she was in
Paris: Living in Paris, a flat in Montmartre. So they'd actually
been in Paris at the same time. She'd walked the streets there
and he'd walked the streets there, with Aka. What if they'd
met? Wasn't that the most awful thought: that one day he
might meet her with someone else! Or that one day she
might meet him with someone else! Both these notions
were his worst nightmares, one was just as bad as the other:
he with someone else, she with someone else; each time he
dwelt on it, and he dwelt on it far too often, it pierced him
so keenly that he was on the verge of passing out, it took
his breath away, and the thought was literally a knife in his
heart, it was so painful that he was amazed at how much
agony a thought could provoke: could a thought affect the
heart and spirit so much that it was lethal? He died a little

each time he thought of Vali, he was a dying man. And he was convinced that if he ever met Vali with someone else, he would collapse in the street.

Heart attack? Stroke? A stroke in the soul, fatal?

What do we die of? I's quietus had a name, and its name was Vali.

I wanted to meet Vali in Oslo, she was in Paris. Only a few days earlier he had walked its streets, with Aka. Perhaps they'd passed Vali, on opposite pavements, going in different directions, in Paris? Was he moving towards a new life? Can one love twice? I didn't think so, and yet he walked with Aka in Paris, their arms around each other, making for a restaurant in Montmartre, sat at a table on the pavement, on the hill, with a view across the city, they kissed, were happy, absorbed in one another; at the same time, on the other side of the street, Vali was walking home: I didn't see her.

I made his way past Oslo docks, heading towards the centre of the city: what did he want there? He wanted nothing there. I couldn't stomach the thought of galleries, art or concerts, theatre or cinema, nor bookshops and publishers, nor friends or the past; everything he generally did in Oslo, all that was dead to him. Vali was Oslo, and Vali was gone, she was in Paris.

They'd lost each other in Paris.

I melted into the crowds of Oslo, he was nobody here. He was nobody and he wanted to go home. He walked to the central station, bought a train ticket and some newspapers, seated himself in a café in the departure hall and waited for the first train home.

I found a seat in the buffet car, ordered two half bottles of wine and wrote in his notebook: Write a novel on a train and don't stop travelling till the book is finished. The novel's title: *The Last Book*, or *The Fortunate Man*. He loves disappearing. He's turned the very act of vanishing into an art form. Like a conjuror. Where the trick is his own death. An old yearning to be invisible. The closest you get to invisibility is travel. The traveller is no one. He who travels is (without realizing it) always imitating that ultimate journey: you're approaching an unknown landscape, you cross the river, and suddenly you don't know where you are, who you are. The oblivion will be total. You won't remember you've been alive, nor do you know you're dead. It must be like finally arriving, returning home to nothing.

I was on his way home, to what? to where? to whom? He drank and felt how well the wine counteracted the swiftness of the journey, as if the speed of the train was slowed, almost eliminated; he sat motionless amongst all that was changing: the landscape which travelled past and was beginning to resemble home; he had no desire to leave the train. Should he take the night train back to Oslo? Extend the journey? He ordered another bottle of wine. Alcohol was always the closest he got to a sort of happiness, a sort of forgetfulness, a sort of presence in the here and now, short-lived, and unreal, not genuine happiness, not genuine forgetfulness, not genuine presence, the intoxication was false, and he loved the falseness that alcohol induced; he could have wished to be drunk all the time. The train had got to Arna. One more tunnel and he'd be in Bergen. It was eight o'clock. He left the train, walked quickly through the city to the nearest watering hole. He ordered a glass of wine at one of the outside tables. He smoked three cigarettes. Then he walked on into the city, along the old Bryggen wharf and up the hill to Øvregaten where he rang Aka's doorbell, and she opened the door.

I was in love, and he wanted to take that love with him to his death. It struck him as a lovely idea: to die when life was at its best. Didn't he want to live with Aka? He did want to live with Aka, but the decision had been made; he kept to it, he lived more lustily because of it, he'd got his life back because of death. Death had given him the best time he'd ever had, and death continued to give him days that were full of vigour: he owed death his death. He couldn't cheat over it. He wanted to live with Aka, to the full, each day, each morning and evening, each and every night. He didn't tell her about his resolution. It was his secret. Death gave him a new life, a new age, he was younger with death hanging over him, as if his impending end gave him a new beginning.

One morning Aka told him that she might be pregnant. They were lying in bed in her little room in town, and she asked if he wanted children, if he wanted to have a child with her? What could he say? He said yes. Perhaps his answer was too pat, she looked at him doubtfully and he said yes. He said yes, I love you and yes, I want a child with you. Perhaps he said yes too many times. Didn't she believe him? He said yes and yes and yes I would, Aka, yes. She began to cry. Don't you want to? he asked. I don't know, she said. Now she held his life in her hands. She said, I don't know. It was as if he hung at the end of a noose, and the noose would neither tighten nor loosen; he hung in mid air, neither dead nor alive. He was dangling in a vacuum, the I-don't-know-vacuum, he had to release or tighten the noose around his neck himself, he said: Yes, I want to, Aka. First you must want to, she said, and then I'll think carefully about it, for both of us, she said. The decision was hers, for the child and for him; two lives were depending on her. She didn't realize it, but she was thinking for three. She thought of a future full of life. Full of possibility. This future child. Which would bring a father into the world. Did she want this? She wasn't sure. She was 33. Hadn't finished her education. There were so many things she wanted to do. Aka was a DJ, an actor, a musician, a poet, what was it she wanted? She had so many talents that it was hard to put all her effort into one, and why should she; she was writing an anthology, directing plays, composing songs, playing dance music in clubs at night, she lived one life during the day and another at night, or was it the same life: I couldn't work Aka out, he who only knew how to do one thing and believed that talent was an obstacle to producing something of value. I was full of prejudice. Aka was full of life. She was beautiful too. She could have anyone she wanted. There were so many she could have; why should she choose one, she who hated choosing, and why should she have a child with I, who was nobody. Aka had to make a decision. She was forced to choose. I had nine months or another new life left to live.

Aka said: June is a lovely name. It blooms and withers. You tell me that you love my hair. Cut it off. Cut me up. You're dazzling me. We belong to the rose family. I love you, I. You give me pain. It does me good. I want to be on my own. Sometimes I want to be with you. Sometimes I need lots of people around me. I need to dance. I need to be loved. Can you love me for two? The smell of blue denim. Brushing your hand across a shirt front. Pressed in amongst bodies. Unable to get out. Being held. I need to be held. If you let me go, I'll be gone. I belong to no one. I belong to everyone. Can you love that? I know who I am. I am Aka. I belong to my name. I wasn't the one who chose the name, I've tried to free myself from it, from the name, from the desire. I'd like to go into a convent. I'm not joking, I want to become someone else. I don't know who I want to be. Perhaps I want to punish myself. I was expecting a breakdown. I imagined a revelation. I wanted to see the world without a body. I lived alone. Built a nunnery inside myself and moved into it. The breakdown came. It's the most painful and valuable thing I've known. Everything went dark. As if someone turned off the light; you must learn to see in the dark. You must learn to see again. I moved to Italy. Light came. Love came. Gradually the world opened up, and I could see it, I walked about Rome and saw: the churches, the paintings, the trees, the swallows, the river, the bridges, the faces, the clothes and my husband: I saw him. I loved. Not just him, but the life we lived, the food we ate, the wine we drank and the friends we met, the places we went to, the music we heard, the plays we saw, the long evenings outside and the days inside, days with books and television and repose. Days of sun and warmth, by the sea, on the beach;

I loved the simple life. I was happy and travelled home. I'm not designed for an easy life, I need to work, to struggle, I need challenges and difficulties, I need resistance, a tougher climate, they're necessary for me to be able to express myself, create something of value. I had to find somewhere that would set my work free; a book, a play, music; I wanted to make something that was mine, that had my voice, my language, my signature. Which was Aka, which was me. I went home. I still haven't found my place. I haven't managed to do my work. I'm in flux. I haven't got enough money. I haven't found enough peace and concentration. I do too many things, a bit here and a bit there. It's as if I'm in lots of pieces, a hand here, a hand there, a mouth here, an ear there, and my eyes somewhere completely different; I want so much to gather all the bits into one body, make them whole again, like sewing a doll together; sewing all the used limbs into a new body: blowing life into it and blowing love into it and there I am! I can't have a child. It's too early. I'm not ready. My body has been sewn up, but it hasn't grown together, there are still stitches and patches and wounds, it isn't mature. I'm more daughter than mother. And you could have been my father.

Aka and I were lovers. They made love, morning and night, outside and in. They made love in toilets and in service areas,

in car parks and in the car: Aka drove wearing a visor and
sunglasses, she wore sportswear and she drove fast, pushed
the car to its limit and cut corners, changed gear and accel-
erated like a rally driver, she overtook, put the car in the
other lane and changed down, revved up and drove past jug-
gernauts and buses; sometimes I would say to himself that's
it we're going to die now, we'll die together, Aka and me.
Aka drove fast and I encouraged her; foot to the floor, he'd
shout. Overtake, he'd shout. Overtake that snail, that rhi-
noceros of a car, overtake the hare, past the fox, overtake the
giraffe and the lion and the leopard; they gave the cars and
articulated lorries animal names and overtook in the jaguar
which was an old SAAB. It's not always the strongest that
survives, said Aka. The wildest live the best. We'll never get
old together, she said. You like Bob Dylan? It's tortoise
music, she said. We need something faster, music with some
tempo and revolution to it, she said. Pull your pants down,
she said. That'll make the car go. I want you so-oo much,
she said. They were driving to Førde. The E39, the new road;
so fresh and newly surfaced, so dark and clean-shaven, said
Aka. And these young tunnels, so moist and wet, they're
dripping, said Aka. Have you ever driven such a wonderful
road, with such easy curves and bends, we'll crash here, she
said and yanked the car off the carriageway, into a rest area.
A real accident, there's no better way to die, would you die
with me? Aka asked. You mustn't joke about it, said I. He

tore off Aka's white tennis blouse. Rolled up her skirt. She kept her sunglasses on and her visor. I expect it looks like we're fighting, she said. I'll bash you with a tennis racket. You hit me with a golf club. We're Hooray Henry and Henrietta, she yelled. We're wallowing in luxury and money, wallowing in excess!

At other times they were poor. Dressed as homeless people, rough sleepers. They walked along the road, on the verge. They hitched. Aka stuck out her thumb. Sometimes she showed them her middle finger. They seldom got lifts. Aka had an accordion strapped to her back with leather straps. She wore a straw hat. An oversized, man's green jacket that had lost its buttons. Pale blue flared trousers. Leather sandals. They had left the car at Sande, at the house of some friends, and were walking to Førde where there was a folk music festival. I carried a rucksack containing sleeping bags and provisions. Bottles of water and wine. They wanted to listen to music. They wanted to sleep outdoors. Just for a few days they wanted to live like tramps, like wandering vagrants. It was a kind of theatre, a travelling show put on by Aka; she liked the thought of living like actors, for a while: some things in life are artificial and some are genuine, it's not that easy to tell one from the other, she said. Sometimes you manage my life, at other times I manage your life, that's how

it is in every relationship; and now you've got to practise
doing what I tell you, she said. It's hard having too much
money, being rich, and it's even harder being poor. It's hard
asking for things. It's hard to beg. I'll teach you to beg, she
said. I'll teach you to be humble. You take yourself too seri-
ously, you're far too secure and comfortable in your own
skin, she said. I'll play the accordion, and you'll sing. We'll
ask for money. If you can't remember the songs, just make
up the verses as you go along. You're a writer. I'm a musician. We depend on each other. We've got no money. You
must learn to improvise. Everything about you is so rigid
and unrhythmical, Aka said to I as they trudged along the
roadside going towards Førde. So controlled and habitual,
you work under a sort of constraint, you're constrained by
routine, said Aka. You do a good job, but there's something
that's more important than good, and that's the thing you
can't control or imagine, the thing that springs out of the
unknown, out of the unfamiliar: we must become strangers.
Even to ourselves. We must become strangers so that we can
produce something new, a new piece of work, a new relationship, a different way of living, I'm expecting something
new from you, said Aka, that's all.

That's quite a lot, said I. He dreaded standing in the street
in Førde singing. He told her so. I hate jazz, he said. I know
you do, she said. You can borrow my hat and sunglasses, and

we'll have some wine, and the song and the lyrics will come pouring out, she said. Aka. Who'd been so quiet, so mute. She'd opened up to him, and now she was full of words. Full of ideas and life. Life which was disturbing I's death. The death he'd decided upon. But he let himself be disturbed. He loved being disturbed by Aka. But could he leave her, and how? The cars swished past. Artics and trailers. Buses and lorries. The road is two totally different environments for the driver and for the pedestrian. The road is beautiful for the driver. The road is hard for the walker. Just a small step the wrong way, a stumble or a trip, and you'll be knocked down and smashed by a metal grille travelling at unconscionable speed; an inhuman force controlled by something humanoid in a car: a face, two hands, feet, accelerator and gear-stick, a body and yet not a whole human being, rather something piecemeal and divided, linked together, half man, half machine in a mechanical body that crushes someone else, as when one animal tears another to pieces, no, that's not the same thing, as when something monstrous and innocent tears something guilty apart: he who stumbles or steps on to the carriageway, he is pulverized and shattered by something shiny, and it's his own fault. The one who dies is the guilty party. He'll lie there destroyed and be responsible for his own death. The driver is innocent. Or heshe is only partly to blame, because heshe is also a part, a part of something bigger, of something smaller, a part of various bits of a machine, of brutality, of power and innocence. This driver, this unknown person, this potential death armour-plated in innocence or partial innocence, there heshe goes driving past, thought I as he trod the asphalt, on the verge heading towards Førde. Just one step to the left and he'd be run over from behind. One step to the left and he'd leave Aka. Happy. Ignorant of everything that wouldn't happen. That wouldn't be. That was impossible anyway. The impossible. The new. What Aka expected of him. It was possible. Just one step away. One step from Aka. To the left. This one step would separate them forever. Would bind them close forever.

Aka was pregnant. It grew within her, this fatherless child. It would be born at the time of I's death. It would be born through I's death. The child would be born with I's death inside it. The child would receive I's death as a birthday present. Was it a present? Its father's absence, yes, that could be a present. A liberation. I could have managed without his father. Just as most children would do better without bad fathers. An absent father is often a good father. A dead father is neither good nor bad. He's not even a memory. Perhaps he's a story. The story of the living father. The father who would never be able to tell his son how he ought to live. What he ought to be. The education he ought to get. The girls he ought to avoid and the makes of car which are decent and the jobs which are necessary and what a good salary is. The son would be spared listening to his father going on about all of this. Maybe his mother will say: your father wanted you to get a good education. But this is a lie, as his father had no thoughts on the subject, he was thought-less. The living father wants a son, but he doesn't want anything to do with that son. He wants his son to be free, father-free. He wants his son to have no father. Perhaps there'll be another man who'll say the things I won't say. Presumably Aka will meet a new man. And this will be beyond I's reach and influence. He won't even be a ghost. He would never have called his son Hamlet.

Aka and I discussed names, they spoke the names aloud, held them out and fitted them up with eyes and mouth, nose and throat; your mother's ears, your father's hands; the way he used to embrace me. The way you'll embrace me one day, like him, your father. Was I a good father? He never told Aka about his decision. It lay there, invisible, almost, like the unborn child, it lay enclosed and secure in I's belly. It grew. Became larger and heavier, took sustenance from I's life and gave sustenance to I's life in those final months. I had a good life in those final months. So good that he'd often decided not to leave it. He wanted to live. He wanted to live with Aka and the child, at the same time as his resolution moved towards its birth with each week and month that passed. In August I read an advertisement in the newspaper that made his decision easier. It was a Cancer Association advert featuring Håvard Aagensen, 51, cancer-free but unwell: 'Living is more than surviving'. Under the headline Håvard explained the effects of the medical treatment that had saved his life, 'the result was that my health was ruined in the effort to save my life'. With subheadings such as Speech, Breathing, Air, Sleep, Work, Håvard gave details of his ailing body and its reduced capacity: 'My ears'. In the past we often used to spend a weekend in Copenhagen as a break from the kids, but with tinnitus I can't cope with a weekend in a big city where there's noise everywhere. And my hearing has really gone downhill after all that radiotherapy. In company I struggle to hear what other people are saying. 'My mouth'. I've got hardly any spit in my mouth, so it dries up straight away. In the mornings my tongue is so dry it can crack. Half my tongue is paralysed and looks really weird. It doesn't work properly, which makes it very hard when you're eating. 'Breathing'. I can't get enough breath. The problem isn't lung capacity. It's the pathways to the lungs that cause the difficulty. They're constricted and always will be, and they're not something I can work on. My nightmare is that my other vocal chord will decide to pack up. Then I really don't know what would happen. 'Speech'. Three years ago I stopped speaking clearly.

I've learnt a few tricks to compensate for this. Whistling and rolling my tongue and stuff like that is totally impossible. 'My eyes'. I've got high pressure on my corneas and cataracts in at least one eye. My vision is getting worse. 'My body'. My hands shake, and the whole of my arms do too, and sometimes my entire body. The worse my health, the more I shake. One injury triggers another. 'My neck'. I need physiotherapy twice a week. Tissues, muscles, tendons—they all seize up without treatment. Then I get cramps and headaches. This leads to all sorts of things: I find it difficult to yawn, for instance. 'My throat'. I'm able to swallow once, but then it's a quarter of an hour before I can swallow again. I can eat anything, but I've got to chew for ages, take a big sip of water, tilt my head back and let it go down, take some more water and hope that nothing gets stuck. 'My nose'. My nose isn't easy to breathe through because of all the scar tissue. I need to irrigate it a couple of times a day. 'Sleep'. I never go to bed until I'm so tired that I'm certain I'll sleep. Lying down is painful, especially for my neck. I have to be sure I'll get off, otherwise the whole night is ruined.

I liked to turn in early. He read in bed. The Cancer Association's piece on Håvard Aagensen left I sleepless. He was terrified of losing his breath, losing his nose, losing his mouth, losing his life, losing his death, his own death. He lay worried and wakeful in bed and thought of his mother. She was also mother to I's decision to die a good death, she'd given birth to his resolution. I's mother had died at the age of 62 when he was 36. She'd smoked since she was 14. I knew her as a beautiful woman and a difficult mother. Difficult because she was headstrong and volatile, always unpredictable; she was extremely temperamental. She was discontented with her life. She had great ambitions for her son. She was an outstandingly gifted person rhetorically. She would often attack her son, launch herself at him, scratching and biting, she fought like a tigress. She had style, she was always fashionably dressed, wore expensive jewellery and watches. She earned her own money, was fond of luxury and travel. She loved lying in the sun. She fretted over her children, they trespassed on her freedom. She was loved by her son. Because he feared her. Because he could never understand her or work her out. Everything of importance that he'd learnt, he'd learnt from having to deal with his mother. What he'd become, he'd become because of her; her strength and resistance, she was his greatest enemy and teacher.

When she was 62, she was diagnosed with lung cancer. She accepted the treatment which was offered to her, the treatment which would destroy her completely. It took two years. Two years of radio- and chemotherapy which turned

her from a human being into a patient. The patient became
a cripple, deathless, so it seemed. She'd been cheated of her
own death. It had been exchanged for the hope of life. For
two years she was a slave to hope and the slow demise doled
out to her by the doctors, more as a penalty than a dignified
end to life. Her punishment was a hope of life. For two years
she was neither a woman, a mother or a spouse, she wasn't
even herself, she was a living corpse, a cancer patient. It was
a metamorphosis. She became unrecognizable. A body that
shrivelled, the way a grape turns into a raisin. She dried out.
She lost weight. She lost her face. She lost her hair and eye-
lashes. She lost her voice. The mother's voice, the woman's
voice, the human voice. She whispered like an automaton.
A puppet. Attached to fragile strings, her movements no
longer her own, she was worked by a cruel hand. Not God's
hand, not death's hand, but the doctor's hand. That cold
hand that attached wires and tubes to her body and fixed
her to cannulas and plastic that bound her to the bed. The
hospital bed. The metal bed in a strange room. White sheets,
white pillows, a white duvet. Not a solitary speck of blood.
Only the bandaged bedsore that grew, that became her. An
increasing wound. An unendurable pain. Dulled with morphine. A drugged disappearance. A drugged death. But at
one point she awoke clear-headed, she asked for a cigarette.
She begged for a cigarette. No one wanted to give her one.
A nicotine patch was stuck on her chest. Her raisin chest.

53

LOVE

There was hardly anything left of her now. Only the practically weightless body on a sheet. Almost floating. Something in her was already floating. It was as if she was in the act of taking off from the bed, and that's what she did, she died and flew away.

I smoked, like his mother, too many cigarettes. He drank too much. He enjoyed drinking. He missed his mother. When he drank, she was there again. She, and all the others who'd died, came back to life again when he'd had a few: when alone I preferred the companionship of the dead. They kept him company. He spoke to people who didn't exist. It was a party. Music and dancing. Rustling dresses. Clinking glasses. Cigarette smoke and white shirt fronts. Jewellery and skin. Coffee tables and runners. Lamps and candlelight. 'Life is but a lamp that is lit and extinguished.' There was singing and impromptu speeches. I recalled something Seneca had said about suicide: 'You can be thrown out of a party, or you can go voluntarily.' There was applause for this. Truth was something the dead understood. They could have wished for better ways to die. They wanted another death. They wanted to have their deaths back. How did you die? I died too suddenly. Another died too painfully and slowly. A third wanted a death surrounded by friends. A fourth wanted to die alone, he died in a hospital ward surrounded by the dying. And the old man, he could have died earlier: age is nothing to covet. And the young boy who'd jumped from a bridge, regretted it. A married couple had taken sleeping pills and were found together in bed. And the dog that never ran off was killed by a car. A friend dropped dead on stage and never managed to say that line from Sophocles: only a fool loves death. An interrupted intercourse, he said her name for the last time and could have wished it was a beginning. The lamp is put out. I had been drinking for several years, ever since the day Vali moved out of the house and he was suddenly alone. Weren't all the cigarettes and alcohol an ongoing party? A slow suicide? It took a long time to drink oneself to death. In the beginning he enjoyed the act of drinking; opening a bottle of wine and emptying it slowly like a cup of poison. It tasted good. It was so good to drink, to fill the mouth with liquid, let it rest there and allow the flavour to seep into the tongue, into the mouth and its blood vessels, the red in the red, so natural, so good, so good to swallow a nice red wine; feel the warmth in the body which received it with heart and kidneys and stomach and liver before it threw the wine up and out over the table he was sitting at, or over the bed he was lying in; all the red sludge he spewed out over the sheets and duvet, table top and papers and everything in the vicinity; he spewed and drank. Made notes and threw up. Smoked and tipped wine into himself, diluting it with water to get the alcohol down and inside his body's wounds; it hurt in his liver and kidneys and stomach. There were pains round his heart. After a few bottles of wine the pains went away. Memories disappeared too, or drink turned them into something harmless and soft, like when you hydrate a dry, hard sponge into a squishy lump; it suited the body's organs so well like a good form of protection and relief, an internal plant or fungus that took away the pain of remembrance; but it needed wetting, needed feeding, and when at last he'd drunk sufficiently and well, he might suddenly sit up in bed or in his chair and say in as loud and candid a voice as he could: It was a good thing she left me!

I lost his appetite for wine, it was alcohol he needed. The pure taste and effect of alcohol, he began to drink spirits. He enjoyed the taste of the alcohol itself; the percentages, the molecules, the chemical liquor; the warmth and sting of spirits. It was like sticking his tongue out towards a flame, taking the flame in, swallowing it and feeling how it suffused his body with reassurance, with peace. A blessed paradox: the flame quenching anxiety. Quenching yearning and loss, quenching sorrow. The flame quenching the flame within him, the desire within him, quenching the life within him. And it was good. It was good to lose yourself, lose your broken heart, lose everything of importance in favour of something that meant nothing; he could sit for hours embracing a lamp. He could lie on the floor caressing a carpet with his hands. He could sit in the wardrobe and tear clothes to shreds. He came into contact with ghosts. He talked to the dead. He found meanings in a book. One world closed and another opened; he grew to love plants and insects. He stared intently at old photographs. Studied the annual rings in a table top. The effects of light on a curtain. He searched for hidden signs showing how everything was connected with everything else, nothing was accidental and everything had a meaning because everything was unimportant; he didn't care about anything. Except the bottles he needed from the off-licence and the cigarettes and ready meals he bought at the local shop. He ordered a taxi, was driven into town and did his shopping there and was driven home like a hunter with his quarry, triumphant, trembling, before he'd opened the first bottle and drunk two glasses in the kitchen listening to the morning news; a cup of coffee, two fried eggs, a slice of bread, keep the food down, don't throw up, drink properly, quickly at first and then slowly, dilute the vodka with orange juice, a little sun, a little sustenance, and later drink the clear spirit neat, until at last he could sit at his writing table, without shaking, to write.

He scribbled the words down, in longhand, in a kind of robotic script, which was illegible. It didn't matter, he was writing. He was carrying on his craft. His trade. An inebriate novel. Written in drink. He would call it: Alcohols. An unreadable novel, at last, he'd dreamt about it: allowing the novel to dissolve, letting it lose its shape by placing the words randomly on the page, letting the words flow over the pages in a language that resembled intoxication, the language of insobriety, he wanted to paint a portrait of drunkenness.

He couldn't make out what he'd written; the letters appeared like unfamiliar runes, the text resembled a foreign language. It was indecipherable and lovely, he thought; the text went flowing across the pages, page after page of seemingly decorative language; occasionally he could make out individual words and meanings in a sentence, the words stood out like boulders in a river, or like the pattern of a carpet, or like shadows in mist, the words vanished and turned up again in a web of text that practically flowed from his biro; a stream of ink. A quantity of liquor. It seemed as if there was a correlation between the spirits and the ink, as when you fill an engine with petrol and give the petrol a spark, a small flame, that was enough, and the text purred and came, all it required was a refill of alcohol. When he was drunk enough, and held the pages up at arm's length and studied the sheets the way you look at a painting, or a watercolour, an amazed and appreciative exclamation would sometimes escape him: The beauty of the letters! The arabesques of the sentences! Language as appearance and disappearance! Oblivion's book!

After several months on spirits he was little more than a body that ached and shook, a head full of obsessions and angst, hands that wouldn't work, feet that wouldn't walk; it was as much as he could do to get out of the house and buy the necessary alcohol; he backed into the taxi, sat in the rear seat with his sunglasses on, it was raining, he hadn't a clue what day it was, which month, March or April, it was Sunday. The off-licence was shut. He had a melt-down, and stood weeping on the city pavement. Should he limp off to Accident & Emergency? Beg to be admitted; a hospital, a psychiatric unit, a detox clinic, anything, he needed help. He found a restaurant. Drank a bottle of wine. Had a bowl of soup. Went on to a bar. Ordered a drink. Knocked it back it quickly. A couple more, and finally his body began to relax, the trembling ceased, his anxiety dissipated and the bar came into focus, took on colour; red wallpaper, embroidered gold flowers on the walls, beautiful lampshades, glinting bottles and the light in the mirror where faces appeared like masks in a cabinet; a half-open mouth, a drinking hand, a closed eye and disjointed sentences and words that floated through the place: No, really. Yes, never. Perhaps not. Who knows. The calm music of soothing voices. Rum and Cola. Vodka and lime. Mojito. Pisco Sour. Bloody Mary. Pina Colada. It was a good bar. Small. Intimate. A couple of leather banquettes, small, round tables and a curved bar. Niko was behind the bar. I had once baby-sat her and her twin brother, they'd lost their father, and at one time he was a kind of surrogate father to the twins. He never considered he was too old to patronize this bar. He was the oldest person here, the majority were young, half his age, he liked young people. Was that a sin? Shameful? He didn't care, he went where he liked, drank where he liked, with whoever he liked. It was his privilege. He was a well-known man. A successful man in the eyes of many. An attractive man in the eyes of some. And then, he had money. He squandered money, spent a lot in the bar, treated people, lent money, gave money away, he liked getting rid of money. And people noticed. Here and there. In the places he frequented. In the places he drank. In the places he ate. The way he never bothered about money. There were always girls around him. Always young men and women in his vicinity. They clustered around him in the bar. Perhaps they wanted a bit of what he had, a touch of fame, some sort of recognition? Perhaps they thought that talent was infectious, something that poured out of him in the form of glittering sentences and brilliant words that lit them up in small, brief flashes, that enlightened them? But he said nothing of consequence. He did nothing of importance. He drank. He was on the way down. Didn't they see that? Didn't they feel pity for him? Wasn't he pathetic? Well, perhaps they found it glamorous watching a well-known man destroying himself in their midst, in their vicinity—because they encouraged him to drink, rejoiced in his mumblings, invited him on to other parties, filled him with alcohol and flattery; it was as if they wanted to help him touch bottom, hasten the end and celebrate it with him, perhaps they wanted to deck themselves out in his decay, in his romantic demise: he was drinking himself to death.

How beautiful they were, these young cannibals.

His male friends. His female friends. He didn't know them. Imma, Joni, Gulo, Arni, Vilje, Eira, Lykke; all these bar room names that blended with the alcohol and raised him up while he was on his way down. He no longer dared to be alone. He drank out, in the city, in various bars. After a certain number of drinks he was buoyant and happy; why couldn't it always be like this; a good, even intoxication in the company of others, often new, sometimes unknown people who entertained him with their hairstyles and clothes, with their glances and voices; lilting, whispering, teasing and reassuring; it was lovely music, he was in good company. After a few months he'd had enough. He couldn't face going out or staying at home; he couldn't bear to be anywhere, and he was tired of drinking, exhausted by hangovers, anxiety-ridden and ill, always worried and sick, unable to read or to write, practically sleepless, without appetite, his nerves taught, never any rest or peace, always the craving to disappear. It was time to leave. He would drink his last bottle of booze and climb the ladder to the attic. Tie the fire rope to a beam. Clamber up on to a stool. Place the noose around his neck. And jump off the stool, into the unknown.

I survived his first death. He slept through it. He woke up in the attic. The sun was shining through the window in the sloping roof. Striking him in the face. He was clutching his mother's fur coat. Threw up into the lining of the coat, crumpled it up; a small animal on the floor. Stinking. Steaming. So full of life. I got to his feet, climbed down the ladder and fumbled his way into the bathroom, got into the shower and stood under the stream of water until he was thoroughly warm. He shaved. Ate a good breakfast and went to bed. He stayed in bed for two days and two nights, sweated and shivered and rolled from side to side on the mattress as if he'd embarked on a sea voyage, he was sailing. I was sailing away in his bed, day and night. The curtain flapped in the breeze. Moonlight and sunshine, wind and stars in an endless night of sea and waves, of thoughts and fears, he rose and sank, let himself lift and fall; rolling from side to side as if in a lifeboat. He was saved. After two days and two nights he managed to get out of bed. He left his bed, walked carefully downstairs to the kitchen. He had bacon and eggs. Drank coffee. Listened to the news on the radio. He got dressed. Clean clothes. Warm jacket, boots. It was March. He went for a long walk by the sea. The reformed drinker knows what time is. What should he fill it with? Alcohol solves the problem of time: the drinker empties his days of it. Drunkenness knows no time of day, or day of the week, it doesn't differentiate between morning and evening, nor does it know the month or season; intoxication is one long season in a cellar without windows, there is no rain or snow. The sun is of little importance. You drink Sunday away. You drink the days away. Intoxication is a foretaste of death, and death knows no time. Timelessness is good. Intoxication is a portent that timelessness is good. The drinker, thought I on the seashore one Sunday in March, knows that death is good.

The drinker empties his life of content, fills his life with meaning. The drinker fills his life with death. Those who have been close to death, know how beautiful life is. And life is beautiful and precious because death has set its mark upon it. The sick will be cured. The dying will live. But I wanted to die. It was this resolution which made his life beautiful. Which filled his last year with meaning.

The summer arrived. I was in love. He was going to be a father. He was writing a book. He was happy. He bore his secret, just as Aka carried her child. We don't know what the child will look like, who the child is, what the child's future will be. We don't know what death looks like, even though we carry it within us all our lives, first as something alien and unwanted, just a small lump, a tumour we don't notice, not even when it grows and has its own inner life. When do we first discern our own death? Is it when you fall down the stairs as a 14-year-old and break your leg, or when you kiss your first girlfriend and know that the relationship will end one day, is it when you get called up for National Service and are trained to take a life, is it when you lose your mother or when your wife dies, no, you won't acknowledge your own death on any of these occasions, it hasn't yet become yours. When does this happen? When is it that you feel death inside you, living there, side by side with what is life, with what is the life inside you?

I knew the first time that the love inside him died. He felt then the black abscess that grew within him. It took more and more room in there, and he could feel it physically as pain. A pain that grew. It was as if the pain consumed everything he was, and he understood that this was death. The pain that grew and the cessation of pain. How the pain would eventually devour itself. It's the beginning of the end. You lead an anaesthetized life, the pain is gone, it's death's presentiment of death. You're no longer living, you're waiting to die. How long will you wait? I feared old age. No, he despised old age. He understood the term vegetable. To vegetate. To wither. To rot. To shrivel. To lose one's vigour, one's feet, one's hands, one's smile. To lose one's lust. One's sexuality. One's beauty. One's hair. To lose one's teeth. To lose one's face. What was old age? A prolonged, constant humiliation. He'd witnessed it, hadn't he? When his philosophy teacher got dementia. He'd sat in a chair at the nursing home and yelled. Shouldn't he have thrown himself out of the window, like Gilles Deleuze? Shouldn't he have died a philosophical death? A venerable death? Shouldn't he have ended his life as it was already gone? Used up? Played out? Fulfilled? Once life is fulfilled, the question isn't how you should live, but how you should die. These were I's thoughts in July, they became even more intense in August and with each passing month. Which was the best way to die? Just as a theatre director visualizes a production, scene by scene, I went through all the various ways to die, death by death, in his mind, first the gentle ways, like swallowing tablets and dying in his sleep, or sitting in the car in the garage, starting the engine and dying behind the wheel, then the tougher ways, like jumping out of a window or off a bridge, or hanging himself somewhere in the house or perhaps in a forest. All these methods had a downside: he would eventually be found. He really wanted to vanish. Was it possible? He didn't like the thought of being found broken and crushed. Even in his thoughts about death I clung to his vanity. He didn't want to set up his death to look like an accident. That would be completely at odds with his intention, which was to die a deliberate death. A longed for death. He wished to die as he had lived; a quiet and happy death.

The winter came. I had decided it was best to die in bed. The last sleep. Would he dream? Would his soul leave his body and fly up to the ceiling? Would he see himself lying in bed? Would he feel pity for himself? Would he regret it? Could the soul feel? Think? See? What was the soul? What did it consist of? And what shape was it? Did it possess his outward appearance, like some spiritual body without organs, without a heart, without breath? Was it just the outer body that died? That lay deathly pale and abandoned on the bed. And if the inner body lived on, as a shade or a spirit,

TOMAS ESPEDAL

and was manifest or visible, so that people could testify that they'd seen a deceased person, perhaps could even speak to him or her, how would he be dressed? Which version of him lived on? Which hairstyle, which face? And would his habits have stuck to him in death? Would he still smoke? Would he still prefer whisky to vodka, Proust to Dostoyevsky? I recalled, from a visit to Mexico, how they buried the departed in his favourite clothes and with his dearest possessions: a knife, his mobile phone, a packet of cigarettes (the cigarettes would run out, and the thought that further supplies would be unavailable, was a nightmare, just as it was in real life, in fact it struck him that these Mexican burial rituals were particularly grizzly, for what was the point of one packet of cigarettes and a half bottle of whisky, other than to prolong the agonies of the deceased?) What was it that endured? A consciousness? A remnant of memory? A recollection that would slowly be erased or mixed with a greater consciousness, a sea of memory, a sea of remembrance? There were so many concepts about death. He would come to a garden, take up residence in a house. Would that be the same house he already lived in? Would he remain in the house, in a different form, as a ghost, a spirit? For how long? Would he see his son being born just the same? Would he be able to touch Aka? Would she feel him as a presence, a faint contact in the dark, an invisible movement in the room, like a current of air, a white, wind-like hand against her hair? While she was having a furtive cigarette on the patio? Would she notice him then? Or would he merely be an inkling, something she imagined in the dark? He was dead. What did that mean? Did he just lie there in his coffin, under the ground, and rot? Was he sucked up by insects and plants and went on living in a different form: a flower, a tree, a worm? Was death beautiful? Was death ugly? Was death evil? Was death good? Was death none of these things, was death nothing? Nothing! Was that possible? Yes, it was. A great, dark nothing! It was possible and it wasn't possible. Perhaps death could be compared to what went before birth. Hadn't there been a long death before life? Had he been nothing then? Or had he lived before, in previous lives? I did imagine sometimes that he'd had previous existences, for example when he heard the music of Christoph Willibald Gluck and a room with dark red wallpaper and heavy curtains, woven carpets and baroque chairs immediately appeared in his mind; an unknown room but one which he knew and moved about in with familiarity, not like in a dream, but as if actually present in a concert chamber; the music started; two violins and a harpsichord: I felt how he was transported from one room to another, from one age to another, from the room where he sat in a leather armchair in 2018, to the room where he now sat next to a woman on a velvet sofa, possibly one of Marie Antoinette's salons, in let's say 1774, it might have been a performance of two trio sonatas in C Major: I recognized some of the faces, as if he was amongst friends, and this recognition wasn't just imagination, but images and impressions the music conjured up for him. Something of the same sort, but in a totally different setting, was the way, whenever he had his hair cut or was in the shower, he'd begin to tremble. The scissors and the shower cubicle aroused the same reaction in him: first he felt a paralysis in his face, and then his head began to shake, slightly, almost imperceptibly, but enough to make him feel uncomfortable and sometimes afraid. I had been together with a Jewish girl at one time, she believed he was a Jew at first, something he hotly denied, almost too hotly and vehemently; he was no Jew, but maybe he'd been one?

Had I been shorn and showered with gas in a concentration camp? I felt it wasn't inconceivable that death encompassed several lives. But it wasn't anything he believed in or lived by, most probably death was the end of everything, at least that was what I hoped. He was neither Christian nor religious; and yet he was unable to free himself from religious thoughts and feelings; he was happy to visit a church, and his bedroom bore evidence of religious symbols: an angel holding two candles, an icon of Mary and the infant Jesus purchased in Greece, a heavy copper crucifix that had been

a gift from the Catholic church in his home town; it was
the thing he would clasp when he had his nightmares. I was
plagued by bad dreams. He could wish himself a believer.
Not that he wanted a heaven or an afterlife, just that a belief
might help him in the here and now, that it might prove
some sort of protection or salvation: I feared evil. Evil visited
him at night, in dreams, but didn't vanish when at last he
awoke, it was in his bedroom in the shape of flying, birdlike
bodies with human faces, he saw them when he was awake,
and reached for the copper crucifix which lay on the bedside table. He wrapped his hands around the cross and said
a kind of prayer, or was it a cry, he prayed for the evil to go
away. Occasionally one of these flies or birds would alight
on his chest, and then he had to fight to keep breathing, to
stay alive, not to die. He didn't want to die like that, involuntarily, forced down into the darkness by a devil or a bird.
He struggled. He wrestled, the way Jacob wrestled with the
angel, he thought in the morning when he awoke on the
far side of the dream, on the right side of the river, as it
seemed to him. He awoke on the life side of the river, of
the dream. He might just as easily have woken up on the
wrong side, on the death side of the dream, of the river, he
thought. He could have died in the dream, his heart could
have stopped, it was pounding wildly in his chest, and his
whole body was paralysed and stiff, it reacted to the dream
as if the dream were death. The dream could have killed

him, but he awoke on the life side of the dream, and for several minutes he had to wrestle with the remnants of death, he had to rekindle life in the body that was dead, that was stiff and unresponsive. Finally he managed to move   an arm. The bird took off from his breast, it flew away and vanished.

I struggled with evil during the day too. He wasn't a good son and he wasn't a good brother or even a good husband. He was glad when his wife had died. He wasn't ashamed of that. He lived a bad life in a bad marriage which he'd adapted to as best he could; I was an unhappy man who embraced unhappiness, almost cultivated it; for years he'd paraded his haplessness and indisposition. Well, that was something! At least he'd never been bored. He was continually plagued by his wife's bad behaviour and infidelity, her lies and linguistic mediocrity; even the way she opened her mouth, the way she shaped it into a pout; it was a mouth that had sucked in and spewed out inanities. Sometimes he thought of her mouth as a public sewer. She liked going to parties and to openings of art exhibitions. She liked being seen at the theatre. She dyed her hair. Used makeup like an air hostess. Dressed in fashionable clothes. She sported hats and jewellery. She was considered a beautiful woman. I laboured under her stupidity and poor taste; suffered from the men she fell for and cuckolded him with. The novels she read. The travels she dreamt of. The wealth she emulated, her lifestyle and turns of phrase, her customs and bad habits; she ate at expensive restaurants and drank the best wines. She was vulgar. Perhaps she was normal. And I allowed himself to be humiliated by her. He tolerated all her accusations and reproaches, he allowed himself to be diminished in her eyes and the eyes of others, he became smaller and smaller and almost dumb; he was in the process of vanishing. He became his wife's adornment, a well-known author who earned the money she lived off, and partied with and used to belittle him. He was her shadow. A dark misfit of a husband. A grumbler. A misanthrope. A humourless critic of the bourgeoisie he'd married into. He was ensnared in idiotic dinner parties and malicious family reunions. He affected a beard. He ate too much and became fat. He was in the process of losing his voice. He couldn't be bothered to speak or to write, the words weren't there for him, and for many years he was the author who didn't write. When Ulla became ill, she lost her beauty and strength. She lost her hair. She developed facial tics and lop-sidedness. Her balance went, and she found difficulty in moving about and walking. She spent more and more time in bed. And I couldn't desert her, no, she needed him. I nursed his wife as though she were his aged mother. He really wanted to make things easier for her, but was glad when at last she was dead. She'd been bedridden for months, she wouldn't go into hospital, she wanted to die at home, in her own bed. I was forced to accompany her towards death. He made her food, fed her, washed her, changed her, read to her and gave her medicine, analgesics. Later on, morphine. She lost the ability to speak and became mute. She lay in bed looking up at the ceiling or out of the window. This was in April. The flowers were blooming and there were white buds on the apple trees. The insects came, the bees arrived and buzzed like electricity in the rhododendron. The wagtail appeared, the blackbird sang. An owl flew past the house. I slept in a bed next to his wife. He heard Ulla crying. Sometimes she screamed. Perhaps she could see death, it came and went in the bedroom. She died in the morning. I was woken by her cries and sat on the edge of her bed, placed his hand on her chest and felt her heart stop beating. He heard her breathing cease. A final, deep breath and then the respiration ended. The warmth left her chest and went from her hands and finally her feet, which turned cold. She became cold. Her face lost its colour, she went white. She became cold and white as the blood stood still within her. The blood stood still and the breath disappeared, it left her, that was how it seemed. As if the breath took itself off and was gone.

I was acquainted with death, it was no stranger to him. He'd felt pity for Ulla when she was ill, and he felt sorrow at her funeral, but after only a few days alone he was overwhelmed by an enormous relief and a feeling of happiness; never before had he felt greater joy. And a few months after Ulla's death he met a younger woman and moved into a flat with her; it was the happiest time of his life.

A new beginning. A new life.

How many times had I experienced this? It felt as if he'd lived several lives, and none of them were alike.

We die several times during the course of a life, and in the space of a few months I went from unhappiness to being happy; he was no longer the same man. After six years Vali left him, and again a part of him died and gave birth to something new: the world weary and grief-stricken man.

He made up his mind to live alone.

To live alone. How do you adapt to it? How do you fill the time? He only knew that he wasn't strong enough to begin another relationship, nor did he want one, he'd rather live a quiet and tranquil life. Could it be a good life? After only a few months, it was during the winter, in November, he was overwhelmed by a leaden weariness. He couldn't get up in the mornings, he just lay in bed. He learnt to sleep for long periods. He woke up early, set to work on the remnants of a dream, tried to lift the dream up out of the darkness and into the light, into the day, so that he could examine it in the half-light like some dimly projected cine film: the images were so brittle and delicate that—if he didn't concentrate hard enough, and it took a lot of effort in the mornings when he risked falling back into uncon-sciousness—the images were constantly on the verge of vanishing, and at any moment he could lose the dream, lose the night and then perhaps he'd lost the key to that door which could open the day, which could tell him what he should do, how he should live, perhaps it was the key to the perfect day?

During this period of fatigue, he taught himself to recall his dreams, the way a photograph is developed, he replaced the night's final image in its liquid darkness, and just as a sentence is made up of words strung together, so the image was joined to other images, to be fished up like a string or roll out of the liquid element that was the dream. The dream produced fleeting images. He learnt to catch hold of them: in the morning, like a relic of the night, a totally different world was shown to him, a world he couldn't possibly have created. A world so distorted and incomprehensible that he lay awake like a Martian or a being from an entirely separate universe.

For a long time he lived in two worlds. He wasn't always able to tell them apart, he lost the ability to distinguish dream from reality. He became a dreamer. He slept himself into a new reality. He woke up then fell back into sleep. Could he summon the dreams? Yes, he could, he had new dreams. He wouldn't get up until two o'clock, and then only reluctantly. He trailed the dreams with him into the kitchen. He sat for long periods staring into space. It wasn't long before he felt tired again, and then he'd lie down on the sofa in the living room. The more he slept, the more tired he was. He was burdened with an overwhelming and all-pervasive exhaustion. He became a sleeper. And he lost interest in the waking world; for the day and all its tasks; he contented himself with eating and dipping into the odd book. He was in the process of fading away.

And someone must have borne false witness against I, because one morning the police phoned even though he'd done nothing wrong. His mobile phone woke him, it was early, and the ring-tone was annoying, because he liked to lie in bed in the mornings. It was like being woken by church bells or birdsong, sounds he'd eliminated by sleeping with the window shut. And nobody ever phoned I in the morning. He'd managed to rid himself of friends to a large extent. There was the rump of a family, but he'd lost touch with them. The voice on the phone was a woman's. It was pleasant. It announced in a calm and sober tone that he was thereby summoned to an interview and that he should attend the police station at Fyllingdal next Monday, the 11th of February, at ten o'clock. He could bring his solicitor. The word solicitor filled him with such misgiving that he immediately decided to cancel the meeting. He thought better of it and suggested a later time. That wasn't acceptable. Then he complained about the distance to the police station, there was one closer, he knew, in the city centre. He was recommended to take the bus, the number 4, and was given an address. He was too tired to make a note of it. Inwardly, in his drowsy being, he'd already decided not to keep the appointment. He didn't like commitments. And he was very touchy about orders and commands. He'd refused National Service. On the other hand, he'd never had any trouble with the police. And he lay there wondering what he could have done to break the law. Was it something he hadn't done? Something he'd neglected, a duty he hadn't fulfilled? He lay sleepless. The more tired he became, the more convinced he was that he was guilty of something, but didn't know what. And because he didn't know what he'd done, the feeling of guilt increased. He lost his appetite. He lost the little he possessed of energy and strength, of spirit; he was becoming ill. He didn't dare go out. Became scared of meeting people. Were they already aware of his crime? Did everybody know? Did everybody know something about him which he didn't know himself? He stopped listening to the radio and reading the papers, these small daily pleasures that had suddenly turned into unreasoning fears. What was it he was scared of? Was he frightened of being exposed? Exposed as what? Deep down in each one of us there lurks a criminal. And now this criminal surfaced in I, he became, in the course of a few days, identical with the guilty party and took over his life entirely. He yearned for a crime. He could have killed. Anyone. The first person he met.

For several days I was the worst of all people: he accused and sentenced himself incessantly for every kind of misconduct.

When Monday finally arrived, he felt glad to be setting out for the police station. He was willing to put his hand up to any sort of crime. He longed for a sentence. He looked forward to facing a concrete accusation. He packed some essentials, changed into a track suit and, with a pack on his back, jogged down to the bus stop. At the police station reception he was met by a young man. I noticed straight away that the young man was nervous. Was the allegation against him that serious? Was the impending offence, the one that hadn't yet been committed, but which would strike like a bolt of lightning within the next hour and become material, according to whether he confessed or managed to refute the charge, was this unperpetrated crime really so grave? The police officer was nervous. It made I relax. He felt he had the upper hand. He had sympathy for the young officer. Being a prosecutor couldn't be pleasant: accusing innocent men, and perhaps even worse, accusing guilty ones. I was shown into a room with two chairs and a small, round table. He was informed that the interview would be filmed and recorded electronically. A report would be written. The young officer was beautiful. Long, fair hair. Gentle, blue eyes. A cautious voice. Shaky to begin with, but more assertive as the conversation progressed. Can you tell us something about yourself? No, I didn't want to say anything about himself. He wanted to hear the allegation. We'll get to that. I just wanted to find out a little about who you are. What you think about yourself. I've done nothing wrong, I said flatly, his words had the definite sound of an admission. What I mean is, I want to know what I'm accused of and by whom. You're accused of sexual assault, the policeman said. The nervousness had gone from his voice, he'd become a prosecutor. He had an allegation. His words were firm and telling, like a blow. A blow to I's entire being, to his whole person, to his whole life and mode of living, to his decency and morality, to his innermost sensitivity and vulnerability: I wasn't and could never be an assailant. A rapist. It wasn't possible. Initially, I felt the anger that all blows elicit, it hurt, but the pain was succeeded by relief. They'd accused the wrong man. Or the accusation was false. And who's made this complaint? I asked. The officer gave the woman's name. It was a name that I cherished. He'd been in love with her. That was seven years ago! I had met her at a literary festival. She'd read his books and said that she had erotic fantasies about him. He was flattered. Curious. At that time he wasn't in a relationship. He fell in love. I was now forced to relate the story of this infatuation to the young officer. It was very unpleasant: having to go over something that had been painful. And the officer was only interested in sexual matters. He explained that I could talk candidly about anything sexual; he was used to hearing things of the worst kind. Nothing, he said, absolutely nothing, he emphasized, was new to him. He'd heard the most sordid things, repeatedly: I would never believe how many assaults and rapes annually, yes monthly, weekly, even daily got reported to him! Most had taken place. Only exceptionally, on rare occasions, were false allegations made. The officer had heard details of the worst and grossest assaults innumerable times, his words hinting that I could divulge his own most salacious doings and peccadilloes. But I was a lover. He had no indecent tastes and hadn't committed any assault. He'd made love to Amy. How on earth was he to explain this to a man who was a specialist in crimes of assault and who perhaps was expecting an admission? Who searched for discrepancies and contradictory accounts, who dug around for signs and traces of inconsistencies in details or behaviour, who attacked the sexual situation from all angles with repeated questions about the most private things. I was a victim in this situation. And he risked having his life destroyed, not simply here and now, but also in what had been his past; since the accusation would cast a lurid light over the person he'd been and the person he was and the person he'd be remembered as; it would define him as a man. The woman who'd accused him, could destroy him as a human being. Was that what she wanted? And why did she want it? The officer asked about any possible motives. It was a difficult question. It was seven years since they'd made love. Amy had had a lover. He knew the relationship had fallen apart, and Amy wrote him an e-mail saying that she'd tried to take her own life and had been admitted to a psychiatric hospital. I regarded the e-mail as an indictment. Was this the accusation she was now levelling again, seven years later? She wanted to absolve her guilt by making him guilty: was this her motive for accusing him of rape? I looked at the officer and reluctantly began to weep. He didn't want to say hard things about Amy. He'd been in love with her: Perhaps she's unbalanced, he said, and she's become ill? I'm sorry, I've no other explanation.

LOVE

The case dragged on. Reports had to be written. More interviews had to be conducted. For several months I lived under a cloud. All it takes for a normal person to change the way he lives is an accusation: he will start behaving abnormally and suspiciously. What had been a normal life-style for I, had now become a suspect lifestyle: didn't he sleep too long in the mornings, and during the day, and didn't he have unwholesome habits, didn't he visit bars in the evening, didn't he seek out the company of young people, and weren't his clothes conspicuously youthful and his language provocative, even brash, wasn't he arrogant and self-important, mendacious and quixotic, intolerant and unrestrained; didn't he deserve punishment? He immediately began administering this punishment: I endlessly monitored and examined his daily activities and innermost thoughts. Was he going mad? Didn't he trust himself any longer? Had he begun to doubt who he was? Wasn't he a good person? Did he have to alter his life completely: was it possible to start a new life, or should he end it once and for all?

I decided to pass sentence. He couldn't bear to wait for the outcome of the investigation. He arranged his living room like a court of law: two chairs, a table. He seated himself in the chair that represented the dock. It was April. The sun shone. Crocuses were out in the garden. First the

crocuses, then the daffodils, then cress, then the dandelions.
The bees came. The wagtail arrived. Snails appeared and the
worms which the thrush pulled out of the ground, it sang
in the morning and in the evening. The buds on the trees
put out leaves, everything around the house turned green.
The grass grew. The lawn needed mowing; I neglected it as
usual. He sat in his living room and rehearsed all the court's
indictments against the accused. The misdeeds of an entire
life were laid bare. Large and small, every last one: everything
had to be dragged into the daylight, the spring daylight; that
merciless judge. I made his speech for the defence. He'd
suddenly become an old man. If anyone in the court could
have held up a mirror, he would have seen the change—
which happened in the course of a few minutes—his face
had crumpled and formed wrinkles under his eyes, the light
in his eyes had gone out, and didn't his hair seem a touch
greyer in the strong spring light? His mouth had developed
a kind of droop, the lower lip opening the mouth like a
question mark; and his neck, hadn't that suddenly bent so
that he was left sitting involuntarily hunched forward as if
someone had placed a stone or some other weight on his
head; this promising head which now dipped a degree
towards his chest, was his breathing more laboured? Was it
a pent up, unhealthy breath that escaped between his teeth,
had he lost a tooth during the proceedings, his mouth felt
wizened and wet; he wept. Judgement was given in the

middle of the day. At two o'clock. It was set down in the record. I noted the judgement as a kind of minute: a few sentences on a sheet of white paper. Then he locked the paper in a drawer, had a cigarette and finally went out into the garden to mow the lawn.

I had made his great decision the previous May. He'd decided he had one year left to live. He'd travelled to France with friends. He'd fallen in love with Aka. She was pregnant. I was going to be a father. He was 56. He had put the past behind him. He had no future. The thing was, the year was running like sand out of an hourglass, time passed so quickly he thought! Couldn't he spin time out, slow it down, yes he could, by concentrating on all the details of the day: its beginning, its middle and its end. Every day had become a holiday. And I tried as hard as he could, in the final months, in the final weeks, to create the perfect day. A day during which he was alert and observant throughout all its phases; from the first rays of the sun in the morning (and, in a fit of early waking, even before that: the end of darkness in that blue hour, a deep blue lit up by the night's last street lamps and stars like pricks of light in a paler blue mixed with the grey of the sea mist; a colour he could actually smell) to the day's end in the evening: a living day! A colourful day! An unsuccessful day (which could be just as important as a successful one). A lost day. The day without birds. The day without trees. The grief-stricken day. The alone day. The Aka day. The day of two joys. The day of books. The walk day. He gave the day many names. The perfect day: a day without worries! A whole day spent with a friend. The day I spent with you. Aka was heavily pregnant. Aka and I walked to the sea, sat on the shore and ate. I threw himself into the cold water. Swam. Do be careful, Aka called; you don't want to get cramp or a heart attack and drown.

Aka was 32. She'd make a good mother. I loved her. He loved the way Aka walked, the way she spoke and laughed, her voice, the way she talked in her sleep. One night he was awoken by her talking, who to, about what, what was this dream, what was she saying, she said, with eyes closed, her breath coming in gasps, so far away, so near in sleep: It's imaginary! Imaginary! She said the word twice and then there was silence. She slept. How beautiful she was. I kissed her forehead. He could never leave her, never, no, he couldn't, wouldn't leave her!

In the final week I began to have doubts. Did he want to die? He'd made up his mind to do it; death had given him his most intense year, death had given him life. And, in a way, he owed death his life. And yet, mightn't it be possible to cheat death? You sell your soul to the devil, but renege on the agreement. You pledge your life to death, and go back on your word. It was possible. It was sensible. It was understandable. You begin to get scared. In the last few weeks, with the end drawing near, I had become frightened of dying. He didn't regret his decision, but now he felt the fear of its consequences, the finality, the death, the great chasm that awaited him. He'd arrived at a place where he loved life. He'd arrived at a place where he didn't want to die; right up close to death; he could glimpse it now, and if death has a face, he could almost see it, and if death has a voice, he could almost hear it; both night and day this dark visage whispered: You can't see me, you can't hear me, but I'm right here, close by you, and soon, quite soon I'll be visible. You will be lit up and darkened. You will tremble and break down. You will repent. You will request a postponement. You will cry out for help. You will plead and weep. You will scream. I will hear you. And I will envelope you. I will thank you. Death needs death to be what it is. Death has got to live too. I will thank I. I am death. I am here, close by, just ahead, almost, soon to be one with you. I and I.

No, I didn't want to die. He wanted to live. It was a warm spring, warmer than usual. The sea temperature was good. I wanted to swim, he would miss the summer. He would miss the autumn, the winter, the snow. He would miss the trees.

He would miss the traffic lights. He would miss going cyc-ling, walking, swimming. He would miss falling asleep and waking up, he would miss the days and the day; he had five days left: Monday, Tuesday, Wednesday, Thursday, Friday, no Saturday, no Sunday, he would miss the Saturdays: the hours spent with coffee and the Saturday papers, the news, the world's miseries, he would miss them. He would miss the Sundays, the evenings with cigarettes and alcohol, he would miss the drink and the music, that deep sense of loneliness and the love songs, the constant refrains, over and over: I love you. I need you. I want you. I miss you. He would miss reading. He would miss his books. The sentences, the words. Those beautiful lines. The smell of paper. The taste of tea. He would miss language. The act of talking. The act of lis-tening. The act of thinking. He would miss his thoughts. Or would he? He'd be dead. He wouldn't miss anything. He'd be free of it all. He would, in just a few days' time, be beyond loss, he would be someone who didn't yearn.

I got a message from a firm on his mobile phone: Unfortunately, we can't find any trace of you on our system.

On Monday I deleted his Facebook page. He deleted all his e-mails, both his inbox and his sent file. He cancelled his subscription to *Klassekampen*.

The hardest thing was to burn all his letters. And his diaries.
I had 52 notebooks filled with diary entries, he burnt them.
It took a whole evening.

What was he to do with all his books? I had a library. He'd
been collecting books since he was 18. He couldn't bear the
thought of moving his books, having to move them out. He
was too cowardly to solve the problem of his books.

He had almost 300,000 kroner in cash in a cupboard in his
bedroom. He put the money in a shoe box and wrote Aka's
name on the top: For Aka.

He left his clothes hanging in the wardrobe.

He put his wrist watch and rings in a tin in the bathroom.

He loved his boots and left them standing in the lobby, as if
ready to go out walking.

He drank, over a couple of evenings, his most expensive
bottles of wine.

He smoked more than 60 cigarettes.

He put the cacti and orchids on a table in the garden.

He wrote a letter to Aka and left it on the desk in the living room.

He couldn't bring himself to burn or throw away the photographs; he'd looked after the family albums and photograph albums, and he'd been taking photos since the age of 19.

On Wednesday he went to Aka's flat in town. He behaved normally. Spent the night with her as usual. Had breakfast and promised to return on Friday: it was two weeks before she was due.

They agreed that the child should be called Simon.

Aka asked what he'd done with his watch and rings. He lied to her. He didn't like lying, but he had to.

I cycled home. He cycled missing his bike already, it was perhaps his dearest possession, apart from his typewriter and camera.

LOVE

I received a packet in the post from Denmark. A small, slim volume from the publishers Brøndum: *Letter in April* by Inger Christensen.

> Then suddenly the light
>
> comes streaming in
>
> and hides us completely.

I spent some hours sitting in the rattan chair gazing at the tulips in his mother's flower vase.

He loved the colour red.

He switched the desk lamp on and off.

He recalled something Aka had said which made a deep impression on him, so deep that it could have altered his life; she said that she'd never killed a fly in her life.

He sat by the window in the living room, and took his leave of all that was inside and out. He was frightened of the following day and lay sleepless that night.

He still hadn't decided where or how he would die.

I didn't sleep that last night. In the morning he got up early, went to the bathroom, and showered and shaved. He ate a good breakfast. He listened to the news on the radio. There were too many birds in the tree outside the kitchen window. He noted that the rhododendron was flowering earlier than usual. It was the hottest May on record. It was Friday. He could hear sounds from the sea; the engine-throb of a freighter, the deep foghorn of the passenger ships. Morning mist, fine weather mist. No clouds. The perfect day. He drank a cup of coffee. Then I went upstairs to his bedroom again, should he go back to bed, no, he opened the wardrobe and put on the best suit he had. White shirt and black tie. He let himself out of the front door and bumped into his neighbour, Rank. As usual, they exchanged a few words. I fetched the lawnmower and cut the communal grass round the terrace. He sweated. He was soaked with sweat. He felt a yearning to go down to the sea, strip off and jump into the cold water. He had 20,000 kroner in cash in his trouser pockets. He could buy whatever he wanted. He could eat well, drink well. He could travel. He took the meandering path down to the sea, through the wood to the flat rocks where a few students were already lying in the sun. He stripped down to his pants and dived from one of the sea rocks. A swallow dive. A brief sensation of flying. Broken by the hard water surface, the cold sea. Vanish under water. Swim. Until your breath gives out, his breath gave out. He swam up to the surface, sunlight struck his face. A couple of terns were flying just above the water. A butterfly perched on a flower in the crack between two rocks. The wind touched the trees, a rustling of leaves. Small, white crests of foam on the waves. I swam towards land. Like an animal, he crawled out of the sea on all fours, out of the seaweed, across the wet, slippery sea rock where he lay in the sun to dry. This could turn into the best day he'd had.

I is searching for a place to die. He walks away from the sea and follows his old school route past the primary school (sounds of break time and the bell which suddenly rings and reminds him of fights in the playground, behind the gym hall; he liked fighting) and round the bends and up the steps towards the mountainside where there's a path leading to the town. There is a place by the river, a clearing in the forest, where he played as a child, where he had his secret hideaway in a fissure in the mountain, an old cave; had it been a sleeping place, a lair for hunters? Once when he'd been hiding in the cave, an eagle flew past and threw a glance at him as he lay on a bed of heather; his blood had frozen and he felt a new fear which must have been an ancient one: the hunter-gatherer's fear of predators, of the wild? Is this the place he's looking for? He goes down on all fours and crawls over the bog, feels how the swamp water seeps into his clothes and makes him wet, makes him feel better, and he crawls on into the narrow cave which is cool and dark. Is this the place? He lies in the cave and gets cold. He wants to feel pain. He wants to be comfortable. He could cut his arteries with a razor blade and lie here and bleed. It'll be hard to find him; and he likes the thought of that; hiding away like an animal and dying like one.

Like an animal. He'd be found by the animals. A fox? A bird? Adders and ants. Insects and vermin. Flies! He's seen animals die. Once during a hike in the mountains, he'd found a dying deer calf, its head covered with flies, they were sucking and boring their way through to the flesh below its forehead and eyes, in its mouth and ears; he'd wiped the flies away with a towel and lifted the calf on to his neck and carried it down to the nearest farm where the farmer had despatched the calf deftly with a knife. He'd like to be found by insect life first, then one day, perhaps, by a hiker's dog. He wants to be found. I already feels how the ants are running about under his suit. He doesn't want to go on lying here. He crawls out of the cave, feels the joy of daylight. It's Friday. He knows only too well it's Friday. The sun is high in the sky. He's still got a whole day at his disposal. He walks towards the river, steps out into the cold, clear water and makes his way up its bed. It's hot, and he's cold. It's good to feel cold, good to feel the coldness in the heat. He leaves the river and finds the path again; follows it up the mountain towards the city that lies ahead, down there. The city! What does he want there? He wants to say goodbye to the streets and some places he's known; a couple of houses, a flat and a few addresses, that's all.

He'll just pop in and out. The city isn't his place. At most it's somewhere to visit and nothing more. A passing-through place. Occasionally a meeting place, a falling-in-love place, also a love-making place and for several years a residential place, but never a settling-down place. Always a transient place. And in recent years practically a non-place. A place he liked less and less until it gradually became a place of annoyances and irritations, almost a hate place. He doesn't like the city. Apart from a few watering holes (where he'd enjoyed himself, in the darkness, in drunkenness: it was almost like being nowhere) and a couple of restaurants, there were no places in town that gave him pleasure, and yet maybe when he was buying from a greengrocer, and when he was walking past a bakery and caught the smell of newly baked bread and saw the woman who stood behind the counter, and those occasions when he bought flowers from a particular florist, and certainly when he caught another glimpse of a special cherry tree, and at other times, of rarer occurrence, when he accidentally bumped into the author who didn't write; the old man with the hat and walking stick, he who belonged to a different age, an age that had vanished, and yet the meeting with the author always breathed life into that vanished time; as if for a few minutes they were part of the nineteenth century and classical literature.

I walks up the gravel track, past three dams, he's following the water up to where it has its source: the crystal-clear mountain lakes. He drinks from the stream. He sits in the shade under a pine tree. It's the perfect day. Is he asleep? Is he dreaming? He sees two women in tracksuits walking past. He hears the birds, tries to tell the different species apart. He read somewhere that Rousseau, during his final illness, wanted to learn the names of all the world's flowers. So hopeless and wonderful! I stands up and walks the last stretch down towards the city. He's singing. Waving his arms. Leaping. Jogging and falling. It's as if he's drunk. Drunk with life. Because he's going to die.

In town I dines at his favourite restaurant. He has a bottle of white wine. He pays by cash. He switches his mobile phone off. He walks through the city. He walks past the flat where his grandparents lived, and the flat where he grew up, next to the park. In the park the students are lying in the sun. Meat and sausages are cooking on disposable barbeques, football is being played on a lawn shaded by trees. Oak trees. Hazels. Beeches. Old trees. Young people. With each passing hour of this final day, I is more and more determined that he will live. He loves life too much to die. He's healthy, he's happy, he's strong. Is he strong enough to die? Is he strong enough to live? To go on. He walks. Automatically now, he walks like a puppet, propelled by strings attached to his hands and feet; he walks towards his resolution, towards his decision; it draws him on. But he can't find the place, his place, the place where he'll end the day. He crosses a footbridge. A young boy dives from the bridge. He turns a somersault in the air. His legs hit the water and he slips under. So simple! So beautiful! I is about to leave the city. He once lived on an island. Is this where he's headed? He walks towards the outskirts; a fast food kiosk, a petrol station, traffic gliding past as he walks on the roadside. Should he turn, walk back the way he came, go home to home? He's tired and longs for his bed, he longs to be able to sleep. The sun is going down, it sinks slowly behind the mountains on the island which is now in sight and gives way to a deeper blue; a hint of black in all that vibrant blue. He loves the colour blue. It's a natural colour, not like red which he associates with textiles and revolt, flags and dresses. Of all colours he likes pink the best. He's always wanted a pink suit. A pair of pink pyjamas. A pink room. Pink is the unfulfilled colour.

I can turn whenever he wants. But he carries on out of town, past swimming baths, a sports complex. How life quietens. Turns quieter outside the city. More peaceful. How people hang around a kiosk. Faces lit up by the motorbikes doing figures of eight on the asphalt square. The hushed high rise blocks. The windows that see: no one here can prevent you from doing what you're going to do. I walks past the residential blocks, past a church which suddenly becomes floodlit. Shining white in the dusk. The graveyard, ranks of tombstones, how the dead lie so neatly in rows.

All these dead names. They live on in the names of others. I's name has many people's deaths within it. I's death will live on in other people's names. As death always lives on in other lives. As something bad or something good. Your death can ruin other people's lives. Your death can be good for other people's lives. It's not impossible. I's death could be good for several people. I's death could be good and bad for others. I's death could be bad for her, for Aka, but it could also be that the absence of a husband and father could be good for the mother and child. It's possible. It's not unusual. I walks up the hill to the next ridge where he stops and lights a cigarette. He feels like a drink. But he must be reasonably sober in the moment of death. He wants to die fully conscious. He wants to see and hear clearly. He wants to register every sight and fear. Perhaps this'll be the most important moment of his life.

It could be the best moment of his life.

He knows nothing about dying. He has no fear of death any more. He knows now where and how it will happen. He smokes and feels calm. It's been the perfect day. He's given the day a final glance, like when you're walking and turn your head and glance behind you and suddenly see the world anew. As if undiscovered. Just as you can sneak a picture of the world at any time: you turn around and catch sight of something you shouldn't have seen! Who is that walking behind you, you see and lose her. You see the sunlight in the tree-tops. You see the birds fly up. You see the world begin.

I wants an entire world with him in an ending. And yet the world will go on, as if nothing had happened, as if normality continues. There is so much death in the world. So much daily death in the world. So many dead, every second; one death is of no more importance than others, than any random death; your death is no more or less important than that of others. And yet the world dies with you, it ceases, for a second or two, like when you hold your breath or make love, the world ceases, before continuing to breathe, continuing to live, without you, without the future that died.

I walks along the side of the road. He's limping. He's weighed down. He's carrying a dwarf on his back. Its weight on his shoulders and the small, wet mouth constantly whispering in his ear: Do it, don't do it! Does no one see that I is unhappy, that he's weighed down? I thrusts out a hand and sticks up his thumb for a lift. He wants to sit in the back of a car. Talk to strangers. Be driven somewhere. Perhaps they'll drive him to a hospital or a police station. But nobody stops. The cars drive past. He sees a fox on the edge of the forest. A crow stares at him from a garden fence. I has always liked being alone, in many ways he's cultivated loneliness and thrived on it; loneliness has been his badge. His otherness. His not-of-this-world feeling. But he's never been so alone as now, he's alone with this choice of his, and he wants to talk to someone about it, anyone, the first person he meets along the road, but he meets no one on the road; there are cars driving past and that's all. There is something in him all the while that wants to turn. He wants to go home. It's too late. He's too far away, too near his destination. And he's too weighed down. The weight has become part of him; he feels tired and heavy, and death will feel like a relief perhaps, like a liberation. That's what he's hoping. A final liberation from the world, a final coalescing with the solitude he's always sought and yearned for. That total solitude. That great silence. The cessation of thought. Of repetition and falsehood. Death must be genuine. Death must be pure. Death must be good. Death must be everything he isn't. Death must be different from everything he knows. Death must be something new. Is there nobody on the road to tell him he's about to make the biggest mistake of his life? I sticks out his hand and hitches. He hears the sound of seagulls. He's getting close to the bridge. The bridge over to the island where he lived alone in an old house for six years: solitude island. In a way he's going home. He knows this stretch. He's walked it before. And each time he crossed the bridge, he thought of his mother. Of how he must have inherited her fear of heights. This heirloom irritated him, the fear of heights, the degree of resemblance to his mother. As he gets to the walkway and out on to the bridge, he has the same old, idiotic thought: perhaps I'll see her again. 'I'll never be able to jump from the bridge.' 'I'll feel your fear of heights and I'll conquer it.'

I goes along the walkway and examines the barrier running alongside, which is a protection against the sea. A lot of people climb over the barrier and jump off the bridge. Everyone on the island knows this. Death is a secret everyone is privy to. I must get out to the middle of the bridge. To the highest point. Then he must wait until there's a gap in the traffic. A couple of minutes, that's all he needs to climb over the barrier. Will he be seen? For a time he'll be standing on the outside of the barrier. Will he wait to be disturbed? A shout, a warning, a rescue? The last thing he'll see, is the town where he was born and where he grew up, the town he loves, it will shine in the darkness. Then he must close his eyes. Overcome his fear of heights, brave life and death, and jump. And in a few final seconds, in the air, he'll be certain to regret it.